I0550426

BEAUTIFULLY WRECKED

CANDIED CRUSH #3

CHARITY PARKERSON

The scanning, uploading, and distributing of this book via the internet or via any other means without the permission of the copyright owner is illegal and punishable by law. Criminal copyright infringement, including infringement without monetary gain, is investigated by the FBI and is punishable by up to 5 years in federal prison and a fine of $250,000. Please purchase only authorized electronic editions, and do not participate in or encourage electronic piracy of copyrighted materials. Brief passages may be quoted for review purposes if credit is given to the copyright holder. Your support of the author's rights is appreciated. Any resemblances to person(s) living or dead, is completely coincidental. All items contained within this novel are products of the author's imagination.

—Warning: This book is intended for readers over the age of 18.

Copyright © 2020 Charity Parkerson
Editor: BZ Hercules Editing & Consultants
Photographer: Pick-your-pic
ISBN: 978-1-946099-73-0
All rights reserved.

❀ Created with Vellum

INTRODUCTION

JOHNNY SEES HIMSELF AS STRAIGHT. WRECKER
DISAGREES. THEIR FRIENDSHIP IS ABOUT TO GET
AN UPGRADE.

When Johnny moved to L.A. to start a singing career, he never expected to end up working instead as security for one of the world's most renowned musicians. It's not so bad. After all, his job led to him meeting his best friend, Wrecker. That's one relationship he wouldn't trade for the world. Johnny just wished he didn't feel quite so strongly about Wrecker, since things are getting awkward.

Wrecker has always wanted Johnny. From the first moment they met, Wrecker has done a horrible job of hiding his interest. He recognizes that he flirts too much, holds eye contact a little too long, and steals touches. The thing is that Johnny lets it go on. Wrecker has a feeling he knows exactly why, and that's why he can't stop.

When an emergency sends Johnny back home to his family, Wrecker tags along for support. Their already perplexing relationship takes a turn when Johnny's family gets the wrong idea. Unfortunately, it's not a move in the direction Wrecker wants. Now Wrecker must choose a path. He can accept Johnny's friendship will never be more or take a chance that Johnny feels the same. Either way, he must choose fast, because Johnny is the type to disappear when things get too hot, and they have been an inferno for way too long.

ONE

THE BACK PORCH WAS LIKE AN EVERYONE-knows-everyone's-name bar, but without the alcohol. Instead, the scent of coffee filled the air of the well-lit coffeehouse. People traveled from table to table, chatting with their friends. They grabbed chairs and pushed tables together when their parties got too big. On Wednesday nights, the place transformed. The lights dimmed and a makeshift stage was brought in. People showcased their talents while everyone else cheered. Johnny understood why people wanted to hang out here. It was a place of positivity and togetherness. Johnny just didn't understand why he —a straight man—wanted to hang out here, since he was the only straight male in the joint. That was a partial lie. Not the straight part. Johnny knew why he was there. Wrecker Lewis.

Wrecker, an ex pro linebacker, who happened to own The Back Porch, was on the list of reasons Johnny started showing up at the coffeehouse on his nights off two months ago. Also, they did karaoke sometimes and Johnny loved that shit. Other than that, Johnny didn't fit in and didn't know why he kept coming back.

Since he had been stopping by every chance he could for a while now, everyone already understood he wasn't looking for a date and left him alone. He was pretty uncomfortable most nights. Still, he kept coming back. He liked Wrecker. Wrecker was different from almost everyone else Johnny had met since moving to L.A. If Wrecker had any personal issues or thought about himself at all, Johnny had never seen it. Wrecker was all about The Back Porch and its patrons. This place was Wrecker's entire life. For some reason that Johnny had yet to decipher, Wrecker's selflessness made Johnny want to know the man's every thought.

The center of Johnny's every thought appeared from nowhere. "What are you doing tomorrow afternoon?" Wrecker asked as he filled the chair across from Johnny.

Johnny blinked at Wrecker's sudden appearance. "Nothing. Why?"

"How do you feel about an afternoon hockey game?"

"Watching or playing?" Johnny asked skeptically. While he didn't mind hitting the gym and did so quite often to stay in shape for work, he did not play sports.

A bright smile lit Wrecker's face. "Watching. I have tickets to tomorrow's game. Would you like to join me?"

Johnny slowly nodded, trying to temper his excitement. "That sounds great. Should I meet you there or at your place?"

"Why don't I pick you up? I haven't been by to see Theo or Ezra in a minute."

"I'll be waiting."

Wrecker glanced around. "Cool. I have to get back to work, but I'll talk to you again before you leave." He started to stand before focusing on Johnny again. "Oh, by the way, I don't know if you actually know him or not, but Brett Sanders was in here looking for you earlier." Wrecker shrugged, as if unsure passing the message along would mean anything to Johnny. "He's friends with Ezra, but he says he met you in Aspen at some club."

A memory sneaked in of a skinny dude with a wild style. "Oh, yeah. I forgot about that guy. When I was trapped in Aspen on Theo and Jessie's honeymoon. We met at Club Incubus. I was thinking it was a small fucking world when I saw him at Ezra and Declan's wedding. He disappeared before I could actually talk to him, though. Why is he looking for me?"

Wrecker shrugged. "He said it was business. I told him I would text him the next time you were in, but I wanted to ask you if that was okay first. I'm not about to be telling people your business if you don't want that."

Johnny couldn't think of a damn thing Brett would want with him, but he wouldn't hide from the guy. "It's cool. I'll hear him out."

With a nod, Wrecker stood. "If you'll be here a few, I'll shoot him a text."

"I'm not going anywhere."

Wrecker touched his arm. Johnny held his breath at the contact and even he didn't know why. Their gazes met and held. Wrecker smirked. "I'll bring you something to drink. On the house."

Johnny might have argued, but there was something wrong with his breathing. Instead, he winked. Johnny didn't realize what he had done until it was too late to take it back. With a smile, Wrecker shook his head and walked away. Johnny forced his eyes away when he realized how his gaze followed Wrecker's every move. It was a mystery to him why Wrecker always made him act weird. Johnny felt good in Wrecker's company. That was all. Of course, that didn't explain why Johnny couldn't stop staring. Even after Wrecker brought him a specialty mocha drink that he always made for Johnny, Johnny's focus stayed locked on the man. He couldn't say how much time passed while he stared at Wrecker, moving from one customer to the next. His wide shoulders took up too much space. Wrecker's t-shirts always protested the size of his biceps. His dark skin looked even darker against the white material.

Johnny forced himself to focus on something else. He sipped his drink. It was cold. Damn. He clearly recalled the steam rising from the cup as Wrecker set it on the table. Johnny didn't get it at all. What was it about Wrecker that distracted him so much? Surely it hadn't been that long since Johnny had a real friend. Was he desperate for human contact? Honestly, he couldn't figure this out. Johnny simply wanted to be in Wrecker's company.

"Hey."

Johnny tore his gaze away from Wrecker for the

millionth time to focus on the pixie-sized guy who appeared at the edge of his table. The man's dark hair was a stylish mess. His checkered suit would have stood out at a circus and his dark blue eyes were focused on Johnny expectantly.

"Hey," Johnny retorted. It might have been a while since he had seen Brett and even longer since they had spoken, but Johnny recognized him. It wasn't like Brett was a forgettable guy. The dude's loud-ass suit begged to be remembered. "It's Brett, right?"

A devilish smile slowly stretched Brett's lips, making Johnny wonder if he practiced the move in the mirror. "You remembered."

Johnny nodded. "Yep. Aspen. I was surprised to see you at Ezra's wedding but didn't get a chance to speak with you."

"I was surprised to hear you sing at Ezra's wedding." Brett motioned toward the empty chair across from Johnny. "May I sit with you?" When Johnny nodded, Brett claimed the seat and kept talking. "I live here in L.A., but I have a major client in Aspen. Falcon Vaspiro."

Johnny blinked. "The famous street fighter?"

A genuine smile snapped to Brett's lips. "Yes. That's the one. Anyhow, I'm his manager slash producer. That's what I do. I make people famous on YouTube. That's also why I was in Aspen. Falcon lives there with his husband, Mason. Honestly, I liked it much better when he lived in Vegas and I could spend time there, hanging out in casinos. For me, there's really nothing to do in Aspen other than visit Club Incubus and freeze my ass off half the year. Snow and skiing. Blah. Anyhow, as I said, I saw you sing at Ezra's wedding. I think you'd be perfect for me. So... would you like to be a star?"

Johnny didn't respond right away. First off, he was too busy trying to catch up because Brett talked too fast. Then Brett's words didn't make sense. Johnny tried working them out. "Are you offering to make me famous?"

Brett's smile grew. "I think it would be a snap. Obviously, Falcon already had stardom before me, since he's been a stuntman for years. But even though Ezra has a famous brother, Ezra had no desire to be famous under his real name, and I had no trouble making him go viral. Plus, those two aren't the only clients I've worked with. Everyone loves beautiful people. You have something special, though. You have natural talent. Not many people have that. Also, you work for Jessie Thunder. You could easily get advice from him on contracting with me. You have a head start on fame already. It would be nothing for me to take you all the way to the top."

Johnny blinked. He couldn't wrap his mind around Brett's offer. "So, you want me to..."

"Sing on camera for money," Brett said, filling in the blanks. "It's really not complicated, sweetie. I come in with a crew and do all the recording, editing, and uploading. Basically, I do all the heavy lifting. Advertising and whatnot. I get forty percent of money generated from anything you do. You get sixty. Ask around. That's more than you'll get from anyone else, considering I'm the only one risking any money on this venture. If you flop, no harm done. You can walk away, but you won't fail. Not with me managing everything."

Johnny opened his mouth. Even he didn't know what he meant to say. Wrecker appeared. He set his hand on Johnny's shoulder and squeezed. All the tension drained from Johnny's body.

"Do you guys need anything?"

"Your opinion," Johnny said without thought, needing his best friend. "Brett says he can make me famous. What do you think?"

"Brett could make a rock famous," Wrecker said without missing a beat. "In your case, though, he won't even have to try. You're an amazing talent.

Everyone would know your name in a week with you two working together. So, I guess, the only question is: do you want to be famous? It's not the prize everyone thinks it is, but if anyone deserves the chance, it's you."

Since Wrecker hadn't hesitated in his answer, and Johnny trusted Wrecker, he didn't need to think about it. "Okay. Just let me know when you want to get started."

The triumph was in Brett's eyes, even if he didn't show it in any other way. "How about tomorrow?"

"I have plans with Wrecker tomorrow." Johnny didn't even need to think about it. He wouldn't break plans with a friend to chase something that would probably never happen.

Brett glanced at his watch. "How about now, then?"

As much as Johnny didn't want to leave yet, he recognized now was a better choice. Wrecker was working and they would be together tomorrow. "That works for me."

Wrecker squeezed Johnny's shoulder again, making him realize Wrecker hadn't stopped touching him. "I have to get back to work."

Johnny glanced up. Unlike usual, Wrecker didn't try to meet his gaze. For some reason Johnny couldn't explain, his chest felt tight over the avoidance. "All right. I'll text you later."

A small smile touched Wrecker's lips. He gave Johnny another light pat on the shoulder before turning away. Johnny watched him go with his heart in his throat. He didn't understand what he had done wrong, but it was like Wrecker withdrew from him more than physically. Johnny turned away, determined to—once again—stop being weird when it came to Wrecker. He found Brett staring at Wrecker too.

Brett's gaze slid his way. He didn't look the least bit guilty for checking out Wrecker. Not that he should. Johnny had zero claim or reason to be jealous. That was ridiculous. "Excuse me," Brett said, coming to his feet. "I just need to talk to Wrecker for a second and then we'll head out."

Johnny fought to keep his expression blank. "Sure thing." By force of will alone, he didn't watch Brett as he headed Wrecker's way. He didn't need to see Wrecker's every reaction to Brett. If Johnny thought about things, he imagined someone like Brett would be Wrecker's type. Brett was pixie-sized and eccentric. He was also too pretty to be a man. The guy had very effeminate features. Brett was the type to stand out in a crowd and catch people's eye.

Johnny could picture Wrecker with someone like that. If he ever pictured him with anyone at all, that is. Johnny blew out a breath.

One day, he would stop being creepy. Seriously. There was no reason for his crazy thoughts. Guys didn't have these thoughts about their friends. Not their male friends anyhow. Fury had Johnny tapping his foot in his impatience. He needed to get laid and it would never happen if he kept hanging out here. Brett had ten minutes and then Johnny was out of there. With or without him. He already had a job he liked. Johnny didn't need Brett's promises of fame. Goddamn it. His gaze slid Wrecker's way again. He did kind of want it, though. Johnny wanted to make Wrecker proud. Fuck. He was a mess.

JOHNNY HAD A STORY LIKE A MILLION OTHERS IN L.A. He had moved to California from Illinois, hoping to make it big. The dude had a voice that could coax the birds from the trees, but—like most people with a dream—that dream hadn't gone anywhere. Instead, Johnny had ended up working for Jessie Thunder. Jessie was one of the greatest drummers in the world. That seemed a solid spot for someone like Johnny to land. Wrecker thought Johnny was happy with his position on Jessie's security team. But now, it seemed the dude would get his shot at fame after all. Wrecker didn't doubt Brett's capabilities at all. If Brett had one talent, it was creating stars. If he had a second, it was making people fall in love with him. He used talent one to feed talent two and that was why Wrecker was so goddamn mad, he wanted to put his fist through a wall.

The moment Wrecker thought he might start breaking glasses and making a scene, Brett appeared behind him. "Boo."

Wrecker ground his back teeth as he turned Brett's way. He didn't bother with pleasantries. "He's straight. Johnny," Wrecker clarified, so there would be no misunderstandings. "Straight as an arrow."

Brett smirked at the claim. "Do you have any idea how many stars I've met who make the same claim? Falcon, for example... You."

Wrecker shook his head. "This is different. Johnny isn't like me. He has no reason to hide. You won't seduce him by dangling his dreams in front of him."

"I'm not dangling," Brett said with a pout. He

looked Johnny's way. "Seriously, though. Look at him. Yum. All that long blond hair and those soulful brown eyes. Just enough scruff on his chin to weaken the knees. The internet will love him."

It really would. God knew Wrecker couldn't take his eyes off him. "What are you looking for from me? Do you want my permission?"

Brett cocked his head to one side and eyed Wrecker like he could see all his secrets. "What is this guy to you? I've never seen you act like this. Back at the table, you couldn't take your eyes off him or move your hand from his shoulder. I'm not trying to seduce him. So what's the story?"

"I'm protecting my friend." Even Wrecker believed the words as they left his mouth.

Brett nodded. "And you believe he needs protecting from me, why?"

"You know why."

A bitter-looking smile pulled at the corners of Brett's mouth. Bitter was the real version of Brett. The version no one ever saw. "Did you ever really love me?"

The straightforwardness of Brett's question shouldn't have surprised him. Brett was always candid. Still, he was somewhat taken aback. That didn't stop him from being honest. "I really wanted to love you."

The way Brett pursed his lips made Wrecker wonder what words Brett swallowed. "Okay." He walked away. Wrecker's chest tightened. Brett might do anything, especially if he suspected Wrecker had feelings for Johnny. Wrecker one hundred percent had feelings for Johnny. He didn't know what they were. They were fresh and brand new. Whatever he felt was dumb as hell, because—as he had pointed out to Brett—Johnny was straight. Johnny was also nice, and he looked at Wrecker in a way that made goosebumps smatter his skin. When Johnny sang, Wrecker felt the music to his soul. Johnny had something special inside him. Wrecker wanted to be near him.

As Wrecker looked on, Brett touched Johnny's shoulder and bent to speak close to his ear. Johnny stood. Johnny's gaze found Wrecker. For a moment, they held each other's stare. Johnny's mouth lifted in one corner—like he knew Wrecker's every thought. Like he knew Wrecker craved his touch. Johnny swiped his long, wavy hair away from his face and pulled it up into a quick bun. He winked before turning away and leaving with Brett. The moment Johnny was out of sight, the spell broke. Wrecker returned to reality. Johnny would never be his. They were no more than friends. That was all they would ever be. He shouldn't care Johnny had left with Brett, except it mattered. Brett knew Wrecker cared about Johnny. No good could come of his ex offering to make Wrecker's current crush into a star. This entire situation made Wrecker want to take a celibacy vow. Sleeping with Brett had been a mistake. One he had made several times until he met Johnny. Now, all Wrecker could do was hope it wasn't a mistake that cost Johnny everything. In truth, Wrecker didn't know what Brett was capable of doing. Brett had always been nice enough, but Wrecker knew what spitefulness could do to a person's life.

Wrecker's phone buzzed, saving his sanity as he realized it was Johnny texting him. He quickly clicked on the message.

Johnny: *I didn't get to stay as long as I wanted tonight. Since Brett has the right set up at his house to record a video tonight, I decided to ride with him to his place. That means I'll be back later to pick up my truck. If you're still there, and I'm sure you will be, you workaholic, I'll help you finish up for the night. Is that cool?*

It was such an odd thing to adore, but Wrecker

loved the way Johnny said all he had to say in one text message. That shit was sexy. Wrecker fucking hated when people texted him fifteen times to relay one message—like he had all goddamn night to stare at his phone while they got to the point. Johnny sending one message felt like an adult move—like the dude understood Wrecker had other shit to do. That was a turn-on.

Wrecker: *Have fun. You'll be awesome. I'll keep an eye out for you.*

Like that, Wrecker was fine. He would get to see Johnny again later. Brett couldn't touch their friendship. Johnny was too amazing for that. They were good.

TWO

Brett's place made Johnny feel like he was always the poor friend. He wasn't a charity case. Johnny's job paid great. Plus, he lived rent free. But damned if everyone he knew wasn't ridiculously wealthy. It was depressing. Like Wrecker taking him to a hockey game tomorrow. Wrecker always did shit like that for Johnny. Johnny wanted to be the one who spoiled Wrecker for once, but in the two months since Ezra got married and they had been hanging out nonstop, Wrecker always beat him to the punch. He paid for everything.

Johnny tried to think of a way to make them even while Brett did some editing. Johnny had sung a popular song unplugged—with no musical accompaniment—to prevent copyright infringement. Brett worked on cleaning it up. Johnny hadn't realized how much work went in to uploading videos. He took his hair down from its bun, rewound it, and put it back up while lost in thoughts of Wrecker. He hoped Wrecker didn't leave the coffeehouse before Johnny made it back. He wanted to help Wrecker clean up.

Brett chuckled. "You remind me of someone when you put your hair up like that."

The way Brett shook his head and smiled had Johnny's curiosity brewing. "Really? Who?"

"This guy, Roman. He's a stripper in Colorado."

Brett definitely had his attention now. "I remind you of a stripper in Colorado," Johnny repeated, trying not to be offended.

A genuine laugh burst from Brett. He looked a hell of a lot nicer when he was being real. "You have the same hair and he's always messing with his: pulling up, taking it down, and then pulling it up again. I mean, I know you're doing it because your hair is on your nerves. For him, it's a show."

Johnny couldn't explain why, but he wanted to know more. "Is it like part of his stripper act, or..."

Brett shook his head. "It's a part of his ego. See,

he gathers his hair." Brett didn't have long hair, but he did a great job of mimicking. "But he makes sure he's flexing hard as he does." Brett flexed his biceps like he checked out his body in a mirror. "And then he pulls his hair up, taking his time and ensuring everyone notices him. It's a show," Brett said, dropping his arms. "He likes the attention. Like, I know you're straight or whatever, but this is a good lesson for anyone of dating age. Don't ever, ever date anyone who is always putting themselves on display. They're always performing, trying to draw all eyes to them with every act. Those are the cheaters. They're not satisfied with one person because they need attention to fill up whatever is missing inside them. I see women do it all the time too. They toss their hair and laugh at jokes that aren't even funny, hoping all heads turn their way. Fall in love with someone who can be still when they're talking to you. Their eyes stay locked on you, focusing on the bubble you're creating together—like no one else exists. Those are the rare gems."

As always, Johnny's mind went straight to Wrecker. Wrecker always sat still and listened when Johnny spoke. Not that they were anything more than friends, but Johnny thought that was probably good advice for making genuine friends too. Johnny tried keeping his mind on topic. "For curiosity's sake, why did you smile so hard while talking about a man who always makes a show of playing with his hair, if he's only feeding his ego?"

Brett smirked and then winked. "It's a very good show." He stood. "Are you ready for me to take you back to your truck?"

Johnny's first reaction was to jump to his feet. Instead, he measured his movements. "Yeah. Thanks for giving me a shot. I can't imagine anyone will want to hear me singing in an empty room with no music, but this was still cool."

Brett rolled his eyes. "You don't have to be modest all the time. You have a great voice and I'm a fantastic producer. Together, we'll be amazing." He led Johnny back down a long hallway past several large rooms. "Tomorrow, I'll talk to Ezra about maybe borrowing Jessie's studio. Obviously, we can't use just any music, because YouTube will strip us of monetization so fast, it'll make your head spin. But you never know. Jessie might have some ideas. What's up with that, by the way?" Brett asked over his shoulder as they headed into the garage. "You work and live with one of the biggest names in music. Why haven't you used that connection to make a name for yourself? If more celebrities were honest, you'd know that's how most people make it big these days. It's all in who you know."

Johnny shrugged, but he didn't answer until he sat in the passenger seat of Brett's Aston Martin. "Obviously, I moved all the way out to L.A., so I was pretty driven when I got here to hit it big. Then I was at this club filled with celebrities with the same thinking as you. I just needed one connection." Johnny turned inside himself, thinking about that night. "Everyone was so beautiful. Unnaturally so. I didn't fit in, which was made even clearer when they refused to let me inside. Still, I watched the stars lingering outside and then I spotted him. The Jessie Thunder. I had idolized his songwriting ability for what felt like forever. He looked untouchable—like a god. From the corner of my eye, I saw this guy headed Jessie's way. There was something about the way he looked at Jessie. It was obvious he meant Jessie harm. I didn't think. I just acted. In a split second, I jumped in front of Jessie as the guy's drink came flying toward him. The glass hit me right in the chest. I was soaked with liquor and the tumbler shattered on impact, slicing through my skin. Like that, I had my connection."

Johnny looked Brett's way and smiled. "Except,

it was Jessie fucking Thunder. I had been a huge fan as long as I could remember, and Jessie turned out to be the nicest, realest person I had met since moving here. Meeting him never turned into making a business connection for me. To me, meeting Jessie was making a connection in life. He's my boss and my friend. That friendship is more important to me than fame. He gave me a job and a place to live. His family became my family. I love him and Ezra. It would break my heart if they ever thought I used them."

"That's... legitimately depressing," Brett said with a chuckle. He made a dismissive motion before Johnny could be offended. "I know Ezra, and Ezra loves you too. He would have helped you in an instant and never thought twice about your motives. That's just who he is, and from what little I know about Jessie, he's the same. Nonetheless, you won't be asking him for any favors. I will, and it's not to use his fame. Just his studio. You'll be great. You'll see."

The Back Porch came into view, and Johnny no longer cared about what happened next with Brett's plan. The lights were still on inside, even though they were closed. That meant Wrecker was still inside. Johnny fought the urge to sit forward and peer closer at the windows. He wanted to see Wrecker.

"You two have an odd friendship," Brett said as he pulled into a parking space next to Johnny's truck.

Johnny cast him a questioning look. "Who? Jessie and me?"

Brett shook his head. "You and Wrecker. Don't take this personally, but Wrecker hasn't had a single straight friend since walking away from football. Straight men haven't exactly treated him well."

Brett seemed to know a lot about Wrecker. Johnny didn't know why that bothered him, but it did. Rather than showing his irritation, Johnny shrugged. "I don't think anyone's sexuality should matter when it comes to friendship. We have a lot in common. That's what friendship is supposed to be about, being around someone who gets your vibe. There's nothing strange about that."

Something Johnny couldn't decipher passed over Brett's face. Brett looked away. "That makes sense. Be careful going home."

Johnny didn't understand what just happened, but he didn't have all night to pick things apart. Wrecker might get away if he waited. "Thanks for everything. Talk to you soon." Without looking back,

Johnny leapt from the car. For some uncomfortable reason he couldn't explain, Johnny didn't head for the building right away. Instead, he opened his driver's side door and pretended to take his time leaving until Brett disappeared from sight. Then he re-locked his truck and made his way to the shop's back door. Wrecker usually left out each night from that door. Light showed around the edge of the door where it was propped slightly open. No doubt Wrecker had been making several trips out with the trash. Johnny slipped inside. The kitchen area smelled fresh and everything sparkled. It looked like Wrecker had been hard at work. When Johnny made his way to the dining area, his steps slowed. He told himself his reaction was due to the wet floor. That didn't explain why his gaze found Wrecker and didn't budge.

With earbuds in his ears, Wrecker danced to the music only he could hear while mopping. Johnny slid into the closest booth to watch. Wrecker had skill. His entire body moved so perfectly that Johnny swore he knew the song Wrecker listened to without hearing a note. Johnny started at Wrecker's feet, taking note of his steps before his gaze traveled upward. Wrecker's bulging thighs strained against his jeans. His ass shook. Johnny took a breath. It was really hot inside the coffeehouse. His gaze refused to move higher. Wrecker turned and Johnny's focus jumped to Wrecker's face. A bright smile waited for him—like Wrecker couldn't be happier to see him. He didn't stop dancing. Johnny was mesmerized as Wrecker danced his way across the room. The way Johnny's cheeks ached told the story of how big his smile grew.

"What are you listening to?" Johnny said the words loud in case the ear buds were noise-cancelling.

Instead of answering, Wrecker plucked one earbud from his ear and stuck it in Johnny's ear. He went back to mopping and dancing as if no one watched him. Johnny couldn't tear his eyes away. The music thumped in his ear. It wasn't a song he recognized, but he knew he would remember it. Something grew inside his chest as he watched Wrecker. Wrecker was shameless and fearless. He was like a ball of sunshine. Johnny didn't know what was missing from his life exactly, but he knew Wrecker filled that spot. Maybe they did have an odd relationship. It was possible Brett was right to question things. That didn't mean they were wrong for each other. Johnny didn't understand what this feeling was when he was with Wrecker, but he knew he didn't want it to stop, because it felt a hell of a lot like happiness. Since Johnny had been missing that for a damn long time, he wouldn't stop coming back for more. All he could do was hope that Wrecker felt the same.

———

IT WAS THE WAY JOHNNY LOOKED AT HIM. THAT was why Wrecker couldn't stop showing out. He doubted Johnny realized his expression. Of course, it was even more likely that Wrecker read too much into things. Johnny probably didn't realize how he looked at Wrecker because he didn't mean the heat in his stare. In fact, what Wrecker took for lust might actually be the strong desire to make Wrecker stop being stupid. Even knowing that, Wrecker kept dancing. He swept the mop across the floor like a partner and shook his hips like he meant to strip. Wrecker didn't know how to stop showing off for Johnny. It was crazy and dumb. None of that mattered, because he liked Johnny. A lot.

The song ended and Wrecker forced himself to stop. The gigantic grin Johnny wore made Wrecker want to keep him that way. He held up one finger and headed for the back. Wrecker put the mop up, washed his hands, and grabbed the stuff he had bought for Johnny right after closing time. He headed back out to the dining room. As he crossed the room, Johnny held his stare. Wrecker took a steadying breath and handed Johnny the bottle of water and a small bag of peanuts. "Peanuts for my favorite nut."

"Fuck yeah," Johnny said, accepting the snack and ignoring Wrecker's innuendo. It was possible he hadn't gotten it, since he didn't see Wrecker that way.

Giving up, Wrecker slid into the booth, sitting across from Johnny. Their feet brushed beneath the table. "What's the story with the peanuts anyhow? I've never seen anyone get so excited over such a bland snack."

Johnny ate a singular peanut before answering. "My mom is a flight attendant," he said with a shrug. "When I was little, she traveled a lot and I didn't get to see her anywhere near as often as I wanted. Anytime I knew she would be coming home, I would wait for her. It didn't matter how late it was before she rolled in, I would be there. She would always kiss me on the forehead and then hand me a few packs of airline peanuts. There were never peanuts in the house otherwise. It was like some magical treat she found just for me." Johnny shrugged again and blushed at the confession. "I was little. I didn't know you could just buy a whole jar at the store. To me, it was like she had gone on a magical journey to find my favorite snack. I had a bit of an imagination, I guess."

"That's adorable." He was adorable, but Wrecker couldn't say that. Instead, he went with a different truth. "As it happens, I did go on a journey to get that treat for you. There's never anything open but gas stations by the time this place closes."

Johnny looked moved by the confession. "You're amazing. Why do you do so much for me?"

Wrecker shrugged. "I like you. Tell me about your dad. I want to hear all your stories."

"He had a lot of affairs and hated me," Johnny said without hesitation, surprising Wrecker. "My parents got divorced when my twin and I were twelve."

"Wait. You have a twin? There're two of you?" Wrecker wanted to see that.

Johnny nodded. "Jenny. She's two minutes older and tells everyone."

Oh, a girl. Wrecker gave a sharp nod. "Jenny. Got it. Parents got divorced. Go on."

Johnny made a dismissive motion. "Dad made a half-assed effort to keep seeing us every other weekend for like six months before calling it quits, which is four months longer than he tried to pay child support. That's it. We never saw him again. The three of us lived with my grandparents so my mom wouldn't have to worry about who would watch us while she worked. That was misery, since my granddad is a grouchy fuck who hates everyone. The minute I turned eighteen, I moved here, and the rest is history."

Wrecker turned the story over in his head, trying to picture the life Johnny painted. Johnny chuckled, snapping Wrecker back to reality. "What?"

Johnny shook his head. "I was just thinking about something Brett said earlier about people sitting still when you talk to them. It hit me anew how right he is."

Wrecker didn't want to talk about Brett, so he didn't dig. "Oh."

"What about you?" Johnny asked before Wrecker could dig deeper into his life. "What are your parents like?"

"I don't know. My grandmama raised me." That

wasn't entirely true. His grandmama had raised him, but he knew what his parents were like. They were leeches.

Johnny pulled a face. "I told you about my mom's magical journey around the world for peanuts and I don't get a single secret."

A chuckle that sounded evil even to him escaped Wrecker. He slid down in his seat until his knees brushed Johnny's. "See, you didn't ask for secrets. I'll have to think about it, if that's what you want." It was possible he had gone too far by bumping knees with Johnny and turning sultry. Johnny visibly retreated.

"I guess 'secret' was the wrong word. I should've said I deserve at least one confession about your childhood."

"I used to paint my toenails because no one ever saw those," Wrecker said before he could take it back.

Johnny solemnly nodded, as if he had been handed a real secret. "Do you still do that?"

Without thought, Wrecker smirked. "Maybe."

Minutes ticked by as they stared at each other in silence. Wrecker spent the time studying Johnny's features. He had the beginnings of a beard. Wrecker wanted to touch it. He wanted to touch Johnny. While staring into Johnny's light brown eyes,

Wrecker pressed his knee to Johnny's again. The corner of Johnny's mouth lifted. Hunger slammed into Wrecker hard enough to steal his breath. He had never wanted anyone as badly. Wrecker couldn't explain it. He honestly didn't think it had anything to do with Johnny not wanting him. This wasn't a case of craving what he couldn't have. Johnny made him feel something. He made Wrecker want to do something other than work. Since losing his football career and his grandmother passed away, Wrecker hadn't cared about anything but his business. Then, this goddamn dude who claimed to be straight had burst into Wrecker's life. Now, he didn't know how to stop wanting him.

"You look ready to go to bed."

Johnny had no fucking idea. Wrecker was beyond ready to go to bed, but not alone. "I probably should."

A flash of something crossed Johnny's features. It was gone before Wrecker could process it. Johnny slid from the booth. "I'll let you get home." He shook the water and peanuts at Wrecker. "Thanks for the snack. I'll buy you a beer at the game tomorrow."

As much as Wrecker wanted to stand and hug Johnny, he knew Johnny wouldn't accept that. Plus, Wrecker was rock hard. There was no hiding what

Johnny did to him. "I look forward to it. I'll pick you up about one so we can find a spot to park."

Johnny nodded. "Sounds good. See you tomorrow."

"See you."

For a moment, Johnny still hesitated before heading for the kitchen to go out the back. Wrecker watched his ass every step of the way. Damn. He was such a beautiful man. Just rugged and handsome. Johnny looked the part of a rockstar's bodyguard. Muscular and fucking perfect. With a sigh, Wrecker stood. As much as Wrecker kept telling himself that his obsession would fade, he knew the truth. This would end with him getting hurt. When he had tried hitting on Johnny at Ezra's wedding, Johnny had told him point blank that he didn't swing that way. Things didn't get any clearer than that. Maybe that was why Wrecker couldn't stop. Johnny was safe. He wouldn't see Johnny's name plastered in the sports headlines next to his. No one would suffer alongside him in his pariah status. Wrecker was free to pretend they were more while not actually being more than friends. That was fucked up. He knew it, but that wouldn't stop him from jacking off tonight with Johnny's name on his lips. Nothing could stop that from happening. Johnny was just too damn sexy to ignore.

JOHNNY DROVE HOME ON AUTOPILOT. HE SWORE he could still feel the pressure of Wrecker's knees pressing against his. Johnny didn't even listen to music in the fifteen minutes it took him to get home. He didn't notice until he pulled into the driveway that he had forgotten to stream his usual playlist. Once inside the garage, Johnny killed the engine and stared at nothing. He tried to keep his mind blank. When that didn't work, he tried going over the few hours he had spent with Brett. Johnny felt... off.

He slipped from the truck and headed for the spiral staircase that led to his loft, overlooking the property. From his many windows, Johnny could see the house and the entire property line. When Declan—the old head of security—married Jessie's brother, Jessie had offered Declan's old bedroom to Johnny. While Johnny didn't have a kitchen in his loft, he had a mini fridge. As far as Johnny could tell, easier access to the kitchen was the only upside to living in the main house. So, he had declined. Johnny liked his privacy. He was especially grateful for it tonight. Confusion had him tied up in knots. He didn't think running into one of the happy couples living in the main house would help matters. After Ezra and Declan married, at first, things hadn't been too bad. With only Jessie and Theo in the main house, Johnny rarely saw anyone. Theo and Jessie never left their bedroom. Then, two weeks ago, Declan and Ezra had decided to accept Jessie's offer to live with him again. Jessie and Ezra needed each other. It made sense for the family to stay together. God knew Jessie's house was big enough. The problem was there was too much happiness in Jessie's house now for someone like Johnny— perpetually alone.

He hadn't felt alone tonight. No matter how hard he tried to quit, Johnny couldn't stop picturing the way Wrecker had focused solely on Johnny. His fascinating eyes had held Johnny captivated for much longer than they should. Then Wrecker had bumped knees with Johnny. Goddamn, he was just... baffled. Without turning on the lights in his loft, Johnny moved to the row of windows overlooking the property and stared out. His gaze slid to the well-lit pool. Ezra and Declan had been married right there. Johnny had sat at Wrecker's side, talking after the ceremony. Their knees had touched then too.

Damn. Why did such a ridiculous thing eat at his brain?

Johnny pressed his forehead to the window and tried to cool his skin. A movement from the corner of his eye caught his attention. He had been so lost in thought that he hadn't realized there was someone at the pool. It was Theo and Jessie. Johnny found himself moving to a closer window to get a better view. A squeal rent the air as Jessie tossed Theo into the water before diving in behind him. Theo came up sputtering and laughing. He fought hard to dunk Jessie, with no luck. Johnny caught himself smiling at the sight of them. Jessie's life had been a mess before a homeless Theo had sneaked into his life. Now they were beautifully in love.

Their playing turned heated. Johnny knew he should move away from the window. Jessie paid him to watch him, but not like this. Whatever they were doing went on beneath the water. That was the excuse Johnny gave himself when he didn't move away. Jessie kissed Theo's neck while Theo clung to him. Clothes flew through the air and landed on the concrete beside the pool. Johnny finally turned away. His dick throbbed. In his heart, he knew it had nothing to do with what went on beneath his window. Johnny moved to the couch and sat. He pulled out his phone and searched for porn. At first, he went with his usual go-to—men fucking flesh lights. He didn't question why that did it for him. It wasn't until Johnny had his dick in his hand and he was too turned on to turn back that he switched his search to men giving head. Johnny couldn't explain his need. His lust skyrocketed. He told himself it was because it was something new and exciting. That didn't explain why he ended up setting the phone aside, closing his eyes, and picturing Wrecker on his knees.

Johnny's breath came out in sharp gasps. He pumped harder and faster. His hips left the couch as he sought the image in his head. Wrecker's lion-like eyes focused on Johnny as he sucked. The pressure beating at his crown blew. Johnny cried out as cum soaked his shirt. He kept beating his cock, unwilling to give up the fantasy until the shame set in. The backs of his eyes burned. He took a deep breath and held it, trying to calm down before a panic attack took hold. It was just thoughts. Fantasies. They didn't matter. No one needed to know. It wasn't like he would ever act on the imagery he used to get off. Johnny liked watching people fuck flesh lights, but he didn't own one. Just because he saw Wrecker in his head didn't mean he would ever let Wrecker get on his knees for him. He would forget this happened and not do this again. It didn't matter Wrecker would never know. They were friends. Johnny's breath came out in a stuttered gasp. He couldn't get the image of Wrecker on his knees out of his head. Fuck it. Johnny closed his eyes and embraced it. He massaged his still semi-hard dick until he got hard again. No one would know. Maybe he would play with his asshole a little this time too. This meant nothing at all.

THREE

WRECKER WOKE WITH HIS DICK STARING UP AT him—like he hadn't been beating on it all night while picturing Johnny's face. This time, he ignored it so he could rush to see the real thing. Since it was Saturday, the coffeehouse would be slammed. That meant Wrecker had to get the place settled to run in his absence for the day. Luckily, one of his regulars—Dawson—had recently started helping out. He looked like he might actually stick around for a while. Wrecker trusted him to take care of things.

With the coffeehouse settled, Wrecker headed to Johnny's place. While Wrecker had been to Jessie's house several times to visit Ezra, he had only been invited to Johnny's loft above the garage once. The day Ezra got married, Johnny had invited Wrecker to tour his nest. Up a spiral staircase and perched high enough to see everything, Johnny had a great view. The place was one huge open room. It seemed Jessie had invited Johnny several times to live inside the main house, but Johnny kept refusing. Wrecker could see it. His loft was peaceful and private—like Johnny.

Unfortunately, Wrecker didn't make it that close to Johnny's bed again. Johnny met him in the driveway before he could climb from his car. Johnny was all smiles as he climbed into the passenger seat. That made everything better.

"Hey. How's it going?"

Wrecker waited until Johnny buckled his seat belt before answering. "I'm good." He put the car in reverse. "You're looking sexy today." He chuckled as he said the words. Wrecker also kept his eyes locked over his shoulder so Johnny wouldn't see how much he really wasn't joking. Johnny looked hot as hell today. His hair fell in waves over his shoulders and his jeans cupped all the right places. Wrecker was a stupid man. Always had been. He never liked anyone he should.

"So do you," Johnny said, laughing.

Wrecker's smile grew. Johnny was fun. Maybe he was straight, but Wrecker's sexuality didn't bother him a bit. If Wrecker wanted to flirt, Johnny would give it right back. The thing was, though, Wrecker had a hard time not reading too much into things. That went back to him always wanting who he couldn't have. It had started in high school with a coach Wrecker couldn't stop crushing on. In fact, that guy was the reason Wrecker had gotten a football scholarship to play for Georgia. Wrecker had never worked so hard for anyone in his life. Then, when Wrecker had gone pro, he had a teammate who made him feel a little too much. The insane part was Wrecker had dated some crazy hot and talented men—like Brett. Anyone would kill to catch Brett's eye. For Wrecker, while he recognized Brett's every amazing quality on an intellectual level, his stupid heart just couldn't love him. Yet two months with Johnny had already completely wrecked his heart and the whole idea was so goddamn dumb. Wrecker couldn't stop. Still, he tried.

All the way to the arena, through getting a few beers and finding their seats, Wrecker kept the talk light. Then, they were in their seats. The too-small area became even smaller with their wide shoulders invading each other's space. Their knees touched.

Wrecker didn't know which of them initiated the contact, but neither of them moved. They were both too tall and muscular to make themselves smaller to fit their space.

Things got underway. Wrecker stood when it seemed like he should stand. He sat when it seemed like he should sit. The whole time, his mind was on every place their bodies touched. Beers came and went. Wrecker had a bad feeling they would be calling for a ride home.

Johnny tapped his thigh and motioned toward the Jumbotron. "You're on the screen." That grabbed Wrecker's attention.

"It looks like we have ex-NFL star Izaak 'Wrecker' Lewis in attendance today."

Wrecker gave a small wave to the camera. Thankfully, it moved on quick. He glanced Johnny's way. Johnny stared back at him, eyeing him in a way that made him feel like Johnny could see all the way to Wrecker's soul. Wrecker flashed him a small smile and went back to watching the game. Sometimes, it was the small things—like being recognized at a hockey game—that punched him in the throat, reminding him of everything he had lost. He swore Johnny had seen that in him in that moment.

Johnny leaned over and spoke close to his ear to

be heard over the crowd. "There's zero chance we're losing this game at this point. Do you want to get out of here?"

Wrecker nodded. "I've got a good buzz going. We should probably head out if we hope to get an Uber."

"I'm good to drive, if you want. I only had that one beer when we first got here. If you're interested, I have a fully stocked liquor cabinet back at my place. We can get shit-faced and you can crash with me."

That was a terrible idea. Wrecker couldn't even begin to stress how horrible of an idea that was. "I'm in."

Johnny's smile made Wrecker wonder how much he would regret this night. Not that it mattered. Wrecker had ruined his life a long time ago. Anything and everything else he did at this point was just icing on the cake.

Two Jack and Cokes into Wrecker staying the night, Johnny started to feel like a mistake had been made. It seemed like Wrecker always sat too close, or hell, maybe he just took up too much space.

Either way, he was right there all the time, smelling too good. It was just that Johnny had seen Wrecker's face when he appeared on that Jumbotron. He swore he felt the loss. Johnny had never achieved his dreams. His hopes of stardom had fizzled out before they had really gotten started. He didn't know what it felt like to have that fame ripped away from him because of something out of his control. Johnny didn't need to personally know how that felt. He had seen it in Wrecker's eyes when the announcers had pointed him out in the crowd. Johnny wanted to fix it.

Wrecker plucked Johnny's empty glass from his hand. "Let me fix you another drink. You need more alcohol in your system. I had way more beers than you at the game. You should get on this same level with me."

A nervous laugh slipped from Johnny as he watched Wrecker pour him another drink. "I don't know. You're a little heavy handed." At his complaint, Wrecker splashed even more liquor in his glass. Johnny suppressed a groan. That didn't stop him from turning it up the second Wrecker passed the glass his way. The liquid burned his throat all the way down and hit like a ton of bricks.

"Goddamn," Johnny breathed through the fire to

the sound of Wrecker's laughter. His head spun. Johnny leaned his head back against the couch and closed his eyes. Wrecker's laughter moved closer. Johnny turned his head and opened his eyes. Wrecker was right there. Inches away. Up close, Wrecker's eyes were even more gorgeous than Johnny believed. They were amber surrounded by whiskey with a hint of green mixed in. "You have awesome eyes."

Wrecker's laughter died. "So do you."

A smile exploded across Johnny's face. "I wasn't saying that just to be saying it. They're really cool. Your eyes are the first thing I noticed about you."

Wrecker's eyes crinkled in the corners as he smiled. "I wasn't saying it just to say it either. Your eyes were the second thing I noticed about you. You're nice. I like spending time with you."

Johnny had always been uncomfortable with praise. He immediately changed the subject. "At the game, when they showed you on the Jumbotron, my first thought was that you should always be like that —up on the screen in front of a huge crowd. Honestly, I don't know much about your football career, but you looked like you belong in the spotlight."

"Yeah, well," Wrecker said with a shrug. "It is what it is, I suppose. I made a lot of money, but I also made a lot of people uncomfortable because of who I am. Why aren't you uncomfortable?"

Wrecker always made Johnny smile. "Why would I be?"

Wrecker shrugged. "We're alone. I'm sitting too close."

Johnny's smile slipped away, but he didn't move. The space between them got even smaller. It got harder to breathe, but Johnny still didn't move. Wrecker came even closer. Johnny's heartbeat pounded in his ears. He couldn't pretend he didn't know what was happening. There was no denying Wrecker was about to kiss him. Johnny didn't know why he didn't stop him, but he kind of wanted to see what happened next. The phone in Johnny's pocket buzzed, startling him back to reality. He leaned away and dug out his phone. His sister's name appeared on the screen. She never called. Jenny was a texter through and through. She hated the phone.

"It's my sister." Even Johnny heard the confusion in his voice as he answered. "Hello?"

"Johnny. It's Jenny. Mom had a heart attack."

Johnny shot to his feet. He didn't know where he

was going, but he felt the instant need to get moving. "What? Is she okay?"

Jenny sniffed. "I don't know. They just took her to the hospital in an ambulance and I'm headed there now."

Johnny glanced around, still searching for a way to do something. "Okay. I'm on my way. I have to book a flight and whatnot, but I'm coming."

Jenny sniffed again. "Thank you. I don't know what to do. I love you."

Johnny's throat swelled. Panic had him in its grip. "I love you too. I'll be there as soon as I can. Just keep me posted."

"I will. I'll let you know." Her voice broke and the terror struck. He disconnected the call and immediately started searching flights.

Wrecker was on his feet too. "What's wrong? What's going on?"

Johnny didn't look his way. "My mom had a heart attack. Jenny is following the ambulance to the hospital. I have to go." He pulled up the flights. "Goddamn it. There's nothing available until like ten o'clock tonight. Fuck. I need to talk to Jessie." His hands shook. There was too much to do and he couldn't think.

"Let me help," Wrecker said, rubbing his back. "I'll go with you."

The amount of immediate relief Johnny felt at Wrecker's offer was immense, but so too was the guilt. "You have your coffee shop. I can't ask you do that."

Wrecker waved off his words. "Don't think about me right now. Go pack a bag and let me handle everything else. I'll talk to Jessie and get us a flight. Let me do this."

As guilty as Johnny felt, he couldn't refuse. Wrecker looked confident and steady. Johnny needed that right now. "Thank you."

A sweet smile touched Wrecker's lips. "Come here." He opened his arms and Johnny didn't hesitate walking into them. His mind was a fucking mess. He was scared shitless and Wrecker was a rock. Johnny didn't take a full breath until Wrecker's arms closed around him. Then Johnny found himself burying his face in the crook of Wrecker's neck and inhaling. It was like he breathed in the man's strength. "I've got you."

Johnny took another steadying breath at the claim. He lifted his head. Wrecker met his gaze. Johnny was still in his arms. It felt like he could let everything go and Wrecker would take charge. He felt like he was falling into Wrecker's eyes, and the next thing he knew, his lips touched Wrecker's. Johnny immediately jumped away, feeling like an ass. "I'm sorry." Heat rushed to his face. "I don't know why I... that was unfair. You didn't deserve that."

Wrecker made a dismissive motion, wiping away Johnny's mistake. "You're under distress right now. Don't worry about me or my feelings, okay? It's fine. Go pack. I've got you."

With a nod, Johnny turned away and headed for his closet. The backs of his eyes burned. He was angry with himself and panicked. Johnny grabbed clothes and slapped them into a suitcase with more force than necessary. He was such an idiot. It was possible he had lost his mom and he had probably just hurt the only real friendship he had by being a complete dumb ass. This was why Johnny kept to himself. He always found a way to overthink things and ruin them.

Wrecker wrapped his arms around Johnny and drew him back against his chest. He touched his lips to the shell of Johnny's ear and inhaled. "Stop. Take a breath."

Johnny took an audible breath. It sounded so loud, it made him realize he had been holding it in.

Wrecker's hold tightened. Johnny took another breath as Wrecker pressed a kiss to his temple. Johnny's muscles relaxed. He knew everything would be okay. Wrecker would take care of him. Johnny had faith.

FOUR

EVERYTHING HAPPENING WAS SO REMINISCENT of Wrecker losing his grandma. She had been his rock, and all he could do was sit around the hospital to wait for her imminent passing. Luckily, Johnny's mom Angie only suffered a mild heart attack. They had put in a stent and would be sending her home before Wrecker and Johnny were even scheduled to fly home themselves. Knowing everything would be fine might have— normally—sent Wrecker into an immediate internal struggle between loyalty to his friend and The Back Porch being temporarily closed. But it was Johnny. There was nowhere else Wrecker would rather be. They had spent their first night in town in a hotel. Since they were both dead on their feet, they had passed out in seconds. No awkward situations at all. When they arrived at Angie's four-bedroom brick home in a middle-class neighborhood, things turned out to be a different story. Once they were under Angie's roof, Jenny refused to let them stay anywhere else.

"Johnny still has a bedroom here. It has a bathroom and everything you two need. There's no sense in you two paying for a hotel room while you're in town."

Since Wrecker was Johnny's guest and Jenny looked too much like Johnny for Wrecker's comfort, Wrecker left Johnny to handle the discussion. Wrecker's lack of knowing what to say wasn't helped by the fact that Johnny's grandparents also lived there. They did not look to be Team Wrecker. In fact, they glared at Wrecker the whole time.

Johnny tried saving him. "It's fine. I can afford a hotel. We don't want to be an extra burden right now."

Jenny rolled her eyes. "Please. Spare me. This is still your home."

"Jenny is right," Johnny's grandmother cut in, eyeing Wrecker—like she wished she could cut him out of the equation. Johnny had her eyes. Wrecker wanted to like her. "Your boyfriend and you should stay. It's sweet seeing you two together, and we never get to see you anymore."

Wrecker almost choked at the misunderstanding. His gaze shot to Johnny. As far as he knew, they hadn't done anything to make anyone think they were together like that, especially since they had been there like five minutes. Between spending all day at the hospital and finding a place for dinner, they hadn't even said anything beyond the introductions to Johnny's grandparents.

Johnny made a dismissive gesture. "No. We're not—"

"Goddamn gays taking over everything," Johnny's grandfather grumbled, sending Wrecker's eyebrows to his hairline. He had thought it seemed weird that the guy hadn't looked pleased since they had arrived, but—more than anything—Wrecker had figured the guy was probably a racist. This was just as bad, and the old dude wasn't done. "It's bad enough Jenny is always over here, flaunting her lesbian ways in our faces. Now Johnny brings his—"

"We'd be happy to stay," Johnny said loudly, drowning out the old man's hate. Johnny turned a worried look Wrecker's way. "Unless you would rather stay in a hotel, which I would completely understand at this point."

"Please don't leave me alone with this," Jenny muttered under her breath.

Wrecker pasted on a faked smile and stepped closer to Johnny's side. "No. We should probably stay here; in case you're needed."

Jenny's gaze swung between them. As her smile and obvious relief grew, so too did Wrecker's boldness. He liked Jenny. She had been really nice to him while they were at the hospital. He wrapped his arm around Johnny's waist. "Should I grab our bags from the car?"

"I'll help." Johnny said, sounding perfectly comfortable with Wrecker's arm around him.

They walked outside the house together. Johnny barely made it out of earshot before exploding. "I'm so, so sorry. If you want me to go back in there and tell them we're not a couple and we're staying in a hotel, I will. I don't know what happened just then. My granddad is awful. He's always been a terrible person and it always brings out the worst in me. I should've warned you."

A chuckle rose in Wrecker's throat. "Stop. Everyone has one old racist, homophobic bastard in their family. Nothing you do or say will change him. I'll be fine."

"But you shouldn't have to just be fine," Johnny

said, yanking his bag from the car with more force than necessary. "You're my guest and you deserve to be treated with respect. I'm just, ugh."

Wrecker couldn't take anymore. Johnny's anger was too adorable. He didn't need any more reasons to fall for Johnny and seeing Johnny's outrage did things to Wrecker's chest. Wrecker took the bag from him before he knocked the wheels off. "It's okay. Calm down."

Johnny took an audible breath and focused on Wrecker. "Thank you for being here with me. I know it's been a huge pain in the ass. Not to mention, being here has taken you away from your coffeehouse to spend time with assholes, but I'm grateful you're here."

Wrecker couldn't help but smile at the description. "I think your sister is very nice."

A smile exploded across Johnny's face. "She thinks you're hot, and she's a lesbian, so you should really take it as a compliment."

A laugh burst from Wrecker. This was why he had volunteered to do this to himself. Moments like these, when Johnny focused on him and nothing else. Wrecker had never felt this connected to anyone. He turned serious. "I'm glad your mom will be okay. We can make it through two nights under the same roof as your family for that miracle."

Johnny's mouth lifted in one corner. "You're really amazing. I don't know if I've ever told you that, but meeting you was a blessing."

Wrecker wanted to kiss him. He hadn't stopped thinking about that small, unintentional kiss Johnny had given him. They were more than friends. Wrecker couldn't help but believe—if Johnny hadn't gotten this horrible news—Johnny would have crossed a line he couldn't uncross after the hockey game. He hadn't forgotten the way they had almost kissed before Johnny's phone had rung. Wrecker also believed Johnny wasn't blind to what was happening between them. Life was rarely black and white. Sexuality was even grayer.

Johnny's gaze dropped to Wrecker's mouth, making Wrecker wonder what he would do next. Wrecker held still and waited. Johnny's tongue swiped across his bottom lip, wetting it. Wrecker fought the urge to close the distance between them and taste the moisture lingering on Johnny's lip. "I guess we should go back inside," Johnny said, sounding absent.

Good humor overcame Wrecker. He truly was a

good seventy percent happier by simply being with Johnny. "We have a bed to share waiting on us."

Johnny's gaze shot to Wrecker's. "Oh, shit. I didn't even think of that. If you want, I can sleep on the floor."

Wrecker rolled his eyes. "That's crazy. We're grown. Wait," he said, hesitating. "Is this a twin-sized bed?"

Johnny laughed as they headed for the door side by side. "No. It's a full, which isn't much better."

"Meh. We'll be all right. I know it'll be hard for you, but I'm sure you can resist my charms for two nights."

Johnny released a mock sigh. "I'll try, but I can't make any promises."

Even though Wrecker laughed, longing had him in a chokehold. Johnny led him inside his bedroom, managing to avoid another run-in with his grandparents. Jenny sat on the bed, waiting for them inside.

She hopped to her feet as they came through the door. "Oh my god, guys. Thank you so much for agreeing to stay. I'm so, so sorry I put you on the spot. There's just no way I can deal with Grandpa on my own."

"We're happy to stay," Wrecker said, speaking up for the both of them.

Relief etched Jenny's features. It was odd seeing Johnny's face—minus the scruff—on a girl. "I wanted to sneak in here and thank you before I hide in my old bedroom for the rest of the night." She kissed Johnny's cheek before hugging Wrecker. "Goodnight, guys. I'm off to FaceTime my super-hot girlfriend so she can make me feel better about my homophobic grandfather."

Wrecker chuckled as she headed for the door. "Goodnight."

Jenny flashed him a smile before peeking her head out the door, as if checking for witnesses. She scurried into the room across the hall before anyone could stop her. Wrecker glanced Johnny's way to share a commiserating look. Instead, he found Johnny watching him with so much heat in his eyes that Wrecker's knees weakened. Wrecker turned away to close the door so Johnny wouldn't see his reaction. On the sly, he locked the door for good measure. They were alone now. With a tiny bed they would have to share. Wrecker could barely breathe.

"You can take the shower first," Johnny offered, pulling Wrecker from a lust-filled spiral. "I doubt there are any toiletries in there, since no one uses this room or bathroom anymore. While you take the bathroom, I'll make the bed."

"You should go first. Just point me in the direction of the pillows and blankets. You're stressed and I'm here to help."

A deep line appeared between Johnny's eyebrows. "Are you sure?"

Wrecker nodded. He wanted that bedroom door locked and that would be ruined if Johnny went in search of sheets.

Johnny motioned absently toward the door. "The door right next to Jenny's room is a linen closet. Grab as little or as much as you want. It doesn't matter to me. As long as I have a pillow and blanket, I'm good."

"I'm on it. You just take care of you."

A gorgeous smile spread across Johnny's face. Wrecker had to draw a steady breath. There was always a small voice in the back of his mind, saying Johnny would never be his. That this was insane and stupid. He definitely should be guarding his heart. Wrecker never did. He just kept falling deeper and deeper, fully believing Johnny would see himself for real someday. Johnny had to know straight men didn't look at Wrecker the way he did. Surely there was a small voice in Johnny's head too. Wrecker wanted to find the side Johnny hid that kept them apart, because he knew they were meant to be together. He felt it in his soul. They were too perfect together for any other outcome. Wrecker just knew it.

JOHNNY COULDN'T LIE. HIS MIND WAS A FUCKING mess. He couldn't explain what happened. Being with Wrecker twenty-four seven was fucking with his head. From the moment he learned his mom would be fine, his brain had shifted gears to completely obsessing about Wrecker and that kiss. Not only the kiss, but the way Wrecker looked at him, always touched him, and the fact that they had almost kissed before Jenny had called interrupting them. Now he had let his family believe they were a couple. It was like he had lost his goddamn mind.

With Wrecker in the shower, Johnny turned into a self-conscious mess. First, he put on pajama pants and crawled beneath the covers. Then he decided he would never sleep in pants. He was uncomfortable and hot. Plus, he was likely overthinking the entire situation. As Wrecker had said, they were grown. There was no reason why they couldn't share a bed and be comfortable. He would sleep in his underwear, the way he always did. No need to pick things apart.

The bathroom door opened. Wrecker stepped out, wearing boxer briefs and nothing else. Johnny's gaze automatically dropped to the huge bulge no one could possibly miss. His heart rate kicked up. Johnny forced his gaze higher. Wrecker's skin looked damp. Johnny took a ragged breath. There was no denying that Wrecker made him hot. No one had to know, and he didn't have to act on his feelings. When he got home, and there was some distance between them, he would take some time to figure himself out. Right now, Johnny felt ten shades of awkward.

Wrecker didn't seem fazed at all. He moved around the room like his entire body wasn't on display, which made sense. They were both men. There was no need to be weird about it. When he turned out the lights, Johnny almost sighed in relief. Then the bed dipped beside him. Wrecker slid beneath the covers. Their arms brushed.

Johnny cleared his throat. "Goodnight."

A deep, sexy rumble of laughter sounded beside him, seeming extra close. "Goodnight."

Johnny stared at the ceiling with his dick painfully hard. Maybe he would never understand why, but he couldn't deny that—for whatever reason

—being close to Wrecker turned him on. His entire body practically vibrated with lust. He couldn't get their kiss out of his head. It had been such a small brush of lips on lips in a moment of distress, but goddamn, Johnny wanted more. He wanted Wrecker. The image of Wrecker's skin, damp from the shower, invaded Johnny's mind. His mouth watered. Every passing second, it got harder to breathe.

Side by side, they both kept their arms crossed over their chests, trying not to touch. The tension in the room was so thick, it choked Johnny. He couldn't stop picturing Wrecker's body. Wrecker was cut like a man who spent hours at the gym every day. Johnny wanted to scream. He was confused and horny. Angry with himself and yet still longing for more. Wrecker was his friend. That was all. His dick leaked inside his underwear, screaming to be touched.

"Johnny, I think I should—"

Johnny pounced. It was like his body exploded into action, making a decision without Johnny's brain, since his head was too stupid to give his body what it wanted. His mouth covered Wrecker's, swallowing whatever the guy had been about to say. Their tongues didn't stroke. They battled. Johnny found himself losing. Wrecker's huge body pinned him to the bed and damned if Johnny's dick didn't twitch like he nearly came with only the pressure of Wrecker's body against his. He bit Wrecker's bottom lip, trying to get closer.

Wrecker drew back, panting. A growl escaped him. Wrecker sat back on his heels and dragged Johnny closer. He tugged and yanked. Cool air brushed his erection as Wrecker peeled his underwear down. Johnny thought maybe he had gone too far. Then Wrecker was back, biting his way down Johnny's chest and stomach. All Johnny could do was gasp and clutch the headboard as Wrecker swallowed his cock. Wrecker was shameless and not the least bit squeamish. Johnny had never been sucked like this. Wrecker sucked Johnny's dick and balls. He licked Johnny's asshole. Johnny had one hand over his mouth, stifling his cries and one hand cracking the wood of the headboard. His hips kept lifting, seeking more. Even when Wrecker had Johnny's whole cock in his throat, Johnny kept trying to get deeper. Johnny was mindless. Despite knowing it was Wrecker, Johnny couldn't think clearly enough anymore to care. He just needed release. His body burned. It had been needing this for way longer than he cared to admit.

Pressure beat at Johnny's crown. His erection throbbed. When the first spasm hit, Wrecker shot upward and covered Johnny's mouth with his. He swallowed Johnny's cries while finishing Johnny off with his hand.

"Shhh," Wrecker said between kisses. "I've got you." Aftershocks rocked Johnny's soul while Wrecker spoke. "You have no idea how much I want you. I want to fuck you. Be inside you. I know you're not ready. You might not ever be, but goddamn, you're wanted. Let me have tonight, okay? You can freak out in the morning, if you'd like, but please let me have tonight."

Johnny didn't need to think about it. Wrecker was wanted too. "It's yours."

"Goddamn," Wrecker growled, making it hard for Johnny to breathe. He moved against Johnny's body—like making love. "I want to slide my dick through your cum, riding your sexy body until I blow. That's how much I want you. I don't care if I can only fuck you like a horny teen. You make me insane." He nipped at Johnny's neck. Johnny's dick twitched—like he was a teenager all over again, getting turned on by everything. Wrecker kept talking and Johnny's lust kept growing, like he hadn't just had the most mind-blowing orgasm of his life.

"You have no idea how many times I've jacked off while chanting your name. Just being near you is a constant tease. Fuck, I really want to be buried in your tight heat." Wrecker shifted positions. He pushed Johnny's thighs apart so his cock could probe at Johnny's asshole. Wrecker didn't try penetrating him. He only toyed with him. "This puckered hole taunts me, begging me to stretch it wide."

Johnny whimpered. His body already begged for more.

Wrecker licked his fingers and circled Johnny's asshole, wetting it. "Do you ever play with yourself like this?" He slipped the tip of his finger inside.

Johnny's hips rose. He bit his lip as a small moan escaped him.

An evil-sounding chuckle rumbled from Wrecker. "Oh, yeah. You know what feels good." Wrecker's finger slid farther inside him. He curled the digit upward and pushed.

A loud pant burst from Johnny. He saw stars. "Oh, god. Please."

Wrecker kissed his chest. "Listen to you, begging so prettily for what I can give you. What will you do for me?" He punctuated his question by massaging the same internal spot, making Johnny writhe.

"Anything. Goddamn. You can have anything."

"Oh, sexy," Wrecker practically purred. "I have a feeling you have no idea what you offer. That's okay. I'll show you." His teeth closed around Johnny's nipple as he went to town, rubbing and massaging. Johnny felt uncomfortably full as more fingers joined the first. He no longer cared. Johnny was mindless. Wrecker owned his body and mind. Johnny was his. Pressure climbed his shaft. Johnny tried touching Wrecker every place he could reach as he shamelessly rode Wrecker's fingers. This was a new feeling, one he couldn't unlearn. When the second orgasm hit, Johnny swore his spirit left his body for a moment. Johnny understood something with perfect clarity in that moment of pure bliss. For whatever reason and without logic, he was completely in love with Wrecker. All the times he had sought Wrecker's company above all others finally made sense.

With his skin sticky with cum in various stages of wet and dry, Johnny came to life. Understanding his feelings gave him power. Made him brave. He needed Wrecker to feel an ounce of the ecstasy Johnny experienced. Otherwise, he had nothing to offer.

"I want to taste you. Can I lick you?"

"Fuck, sexy. You can do whatever you want to me."

With Wrecker sitting on the bed, Johnny shifted until his head was in Wrecker's lap. He had no idea what to do. His emotions were in charge. He didn't think. Johnny just licked, lapping at Wrecker's wet crown. Wrecker gently held his hair while Johnny explored. No doubt it was the ineptest service Wrecker had ever gotten. All Johnny had was heart. This wasn't about anything but Johnny wanting to know what Wrecker's dick would feel like in his mouth. He licked and sucked, savoring the newness of the experience. Wrecker tasted salty. He made sounds like he enjoyed the process. Johnny let those moans lead him. Wrecker had a huge cock. Johnny didn't try to do the tricks Wrecker had done. He simply stroked Wrecker's shaft while sucking his crown.

"Holy shit, Johnny. You make my mind a mess." Wrecker started panting like he might blow any second. His hips gently rocked upward, matching the rhythm of Johnny's motions. He didn't try forcing Johnny to take more of him. Wrecker accepted what Johnny gave. Johnny didn't have time to decide if he was the type to spit or swallow. Hot cum filled his mouth and Johnny automatically swallowed without thought. "Oh, shit. Goddamn, Johnny. That's fucking hot. I can't believe you did that. Fuck me.

You really drank my cum. Come here. Let me taste it." He dragged Johnny's mouth to his. Their kiss was almost primal. Wrecker ate at Johnny's mouth, sucking on his tongue—like he tried taking his cum back. Wrecker moved and pushed until his body covered Johnny's again. His kiss turned reverent. Johnny found himself clinging to Wrecker, seeking more.

"Dear god," Wrecker whispered as he changed angles. "Please don't regret me in the morning. It'll kill me if you regret me."

Johnny didn't know what the morning would bring. All he knew was how he felt now—like something beautiful had just happened. Johnny didn't want to lose this feeling, so he would try to embrace it. Wrecker had already been the one person he couldn't live without before this happened. He didn't think that could change. All Johnny could do was give this his best shot. Damn, he really hoped Wrecker didn't regret him either.

FIVE

It was a beautiful day. Johnny's mom was on the mend. He had woken up next to Wrecker. Things felt good—like he would be okay. While he didn't know where things were headed with Wrecker, Johnny had decided not to overthink anything. Wrecker didn't strike him as someone looking for a relationship. There was no reason for him to borrow trouble. For now, they could just sort of see where things went. He could handle that.

Johnny took a deep breath, taking in the fresh air. He had grown up in this neighborhood. It was quiet, consisting of mostly families and the elderly. Jenny and he had run the roads and played with all the neighborhood kids. Jenny had always fit in a little better than Johnny. That was pretty much the whole story of Johnny's life. Even if the most popular crowd invited him places, he sat on the fringes, feeling like a fraud. He had always been certain every single person he met didn't really like him, no matter how nice they were. Johnny was a square peg in a round world. Nothing about him was the same as anyone else. When he was with Wrecker, that was the only time Johnny felt like he could relax. Wrecker made Johnny believe he had a real friend.

The back door opened, and his mom stepped out. Her long blonde hair had a lot more gray in it than he remembered. Jenny had picked her up from the hospital early that morning. She hadn't relaxed yet, which didn't surprise Johnny at all.

She flashed him a smile and moved to sit next to him on the patio stairs, leading to the backyard. "Hey, baby."

Johnny kissed her cheek. "You're supposed to be in bed."

She made a noncommittal sound and took a drink of the water she held. "You're still young. You have no idea how much it hurts to stay in bed all day. My back hurts in three places and my hips are killing me. It can't be helping my heart to be in constant pain. I'll be fine."

Johnny shook his head. She was exasperating.

Always had been. "You couldn't humor me for one day. I'm leaving tomorrow. You could've stayed in your room and I never would've known you had no intention of following your doctor's orders."

She shrugged. "I'm sure I'll get tired and go back to bed soon. Right now, though, I want to sit with my son. So stop bitching."

The back door opened again, and his grandfather stepped out. Johnny nearly groaned. He couldn't have five minutes alone with his mom.

"Are you taking this time to tell your mother how you've disappointed the family... again?"

Johnny rolled his eyes and sipped his coffee while playing deaf. No good could come of engaging. His grandfather had always been like this—a cranky and mean fuck, even before he got old.

Angie pat his knee. "You know I'm proud as hell of you. It's impossible for you to disappoint me."

Johnny flashed her a smile.

Jenny stepped out with Wrecker in tow. They were laughing. Jenny's smile slipped away as she spotted their grandfather. He could tell she tried to decide whether to stay. Wrecker's gaze latched on to Johnny's with so much heat that Johnny had to take a steadying breath. Every second of last night kept running through his mind, torturing him with a desire for more.

His grandfather huffed. "Great. You're still here."

A small growl escaped Jenny. "Stuff it, old man. My mom lives here. I'll be here if I want."

"I was talking to the boy. He's got a lot of nerve staying under our roof."

Johnny covered his eyes. This was like being trapped in hell.

"Stop it, Dad." His mom's interventions never worked. This time was no different.

"This is my house. I'll say what I want. He's not welcome here."

Johnny turned, ready to blast him.

Wrecker leveled a steady stare upon Johnny's grandfather. He looked calm and unflappable. "Since I'm here for Johnny, he can be the one to tell me to go. I wish you would think of him rather than your hatred. I make your grandson happy."

He really did. Johnny's chest swelled with pride. Wrecker was much calmer than Johnny wanted to be.

His grandfather snorted. His hard and disbelieving gaze landed on Wrecker. "Do you? Because I can't imagine he'll be too happy when you destroy his dream career the way you did your own by choosing this gay thing. It's only a matter of time before Johnny takes the world by storm. He has real talent. You'll be a fucking embarrassment when that day comes."

"Oh, for fuck's sake," Jenny said, speaking up. "You need to stop. Johnny is a grown man and Wrecker is good to him. You need to learn to set your hate aside—"

"It's not right," his grandfather yelled, banging his cane on the wooden patio. "The Bible says—"

"Fuck what the Bible says," Jenny yelled over the top of him. "That book says a lot of things that you don't follow. Johnny is allowed—"

Johnny stood. "Goddamn it. Just stop. This has gotten way out of hand. I'm not gay, okay? Wrecker is my best friend. You guys just assumed we're dating, and I let you think it because Grandpa was treating Jenny like shit. The way he always does, and I'd had enough. We're not dating."

His grandfather wasn't letting it go. "I'm not stupid. I've always known you're gay. Don't play that BS."

"I am not gay. We're not dating." Johnny yelled the words at the top of his lungs—like a complete lunatic.

Wrecker dropped his gaze to the cup of coffee he held. A self-deprecating smile touched his lips as he shook his head and looked away. Johnny realized too late how his outburst must have sounded to Wrecker. He had literally screamed the denial, taking back every intimate moment between them. Before Johnny could think of what to do, Wrecker walked away, heading back inside.

Angie pointed at the car. "Johnny Wayne Savage, get in the car. We're going for a drive."

Johnny snorted, his temper completely gone. Wrecker had walked away from him, and everyone was yelling. Johnny was fed up, the way he had always been before finally walking away from this bullshit nine years ago. "I'm too old for car rides where you lecture me while I can't get away. Say what you plan to say."

"Get in the goddamn car," Angie screamed, coming completely unglued.

"Mom, calm down," Jenny said, stepping in. "Johnny is getting in the car. I'll drive, though. You're supposed to be resting."

At the reality check of why they were all there, Johnny headed for the car. The last thing he wanted was to be responsible for his mom's death. She was supposed to be calm and resting. He wouldn't make her stand in the yard, screaming at him. It wasn't her fault that none of them had ever been able to get along.

With his seat belt in place and the tension high, they barely made it out of the driveway before his mom started. "What in the hell was that, Johnny? You bring that boy to my house and humiliate him like that. That's not right. To top things off, you yell at your granddaddy."

Johnny turned in his seat, immediately forgetting he had just decided not to stress out his mom. "That might be your dad, but that doesn't make him shit to me. He treats Jenny like shit because of who she is, and that's not right. I was done with him a long time ago. You might feel obligated to him, but I don't. I came here for you."

His mom's light brown eyes flashed with fire. "Stop avoiding what you just did. This isn't about your grandfather. That sweet guy came here with you, sat by your side, and looks at you like you hung the moon. How could you do what you just did?"

A humorless laugh escaped Johnny. "Mom, I'm not—"

"I swear by all that's holy, if you say you're not gay to me again, I will slap you into next year," his mom threatened. "This has nothing to do with labels.

This is about how you two look at each other. Not everyone gets that. Not everyone has someone who cares enough about them to drop everything to come across the country to practically be spit on by a bitter old man."

Johnny started to interrupt.

His mom slashed her hand through the air, cutting him off again. "Just listen. I almost died." That was a low blow to shut him up, but it worked. "Life is short, Johnny. Stop listening to your dad's voice in your head, telling you stop holding boys' hands."

Johnny turned away and stared at the road. That one hurt. He was done listening to this. "I should get back to Wrecker. No doubt Grandpa has started in about the color of his skin now that we're not there to stop it from happening."

With a huff, his mom leaned back in her seat and crossed her arms over her chest. "When we get back to the house, I expect you to apologize to Wrecker. That was inexcusable. I don't care what you're telling yourself, but it matters what you just did to him."

Goddamn it. Did she really think he didn't know that? Nothing mattered to him as much as Wrecker. He never would have said what he said if he had been thinking straight. Johnny had lost his temper and gotten uncomfortable. He had never been good at dealing with people yelling.

The moment Jenny pulled back into the driveway, Johnny was out. He climbed the stairs to where his grandparents still sat. Johnny didn't as much as look their way. While his grandmother had always been good to him, her silence while Johnny got constantly berated was just as unforgivable. Johnny wouldn't forget why he had left this town behind again. Inside the house, there was no sign of Wrecker. He headed for the bedroom. Wrecker's suitcase was gone. With a growl, Johnny rushed back outside.

"Where did Wrecker go?"

No one answered.

A growl of frustration rose in Johnny's throat. He didn't understand how he had come from these people, and they wondered why he never brought anyone home to meet them. The thought gave Johnny pause. There hadn't been anyone to bring home. Wrecker was it. He was the only one who had ever meant anything to him, and Johnny had lost him. In the blink of an eye with the smallest burst of temper, Wrecker was gone. Johnny had no clue what to do now.

THE DAY HAD STARTED SO BEAUTIFULLY. IN FACT, when Wrecker woke this morning, he hadn't stopped smiling until the shit hit the fan. He could still feel Johnny's body beneath him. Unfortunately, Wrecker could also still hear Johnny's denials ringing in his ears. Johnny had been adamant. He had known himself in the moment he had refuted being in a relationship with Wrecker. Wrecker had seen the surety in Johnny's eyes. Staying in Illinois would only be postponing the inevitable. Johnny might feel something for Wrecker, but whatever he felt wasn't enough to actually be with Wrecker—like a real couple. Just like Wrecker had been with his football team, Wrecker was an embarrassment to Johnny. Wrecker hadn't stood for that bullshit with them and he wouldn't do it for Johnny.

"It's a shame no team would pick you up after you came out. You were a lot of fun to watch."

Wrecker tried for a smile. It was hardly the guy working the ticket counter at the airport's fault that Wrecker's life was complete bullshit. "Thanks for that. I miss playing."

The guy clicked around on his computer but

kept up his end of the conversation. "What do you do now?"

Wrecker's cellphone rang for the hundredth time since leaving Johnny behind. Johnny's name flashed across the screen. Wrecker turned off the device. "I own a coffeehouse in L.A. It's a lot more work for a lot less pay, but it's still a dream come true." Even Wrecker heard the bitterness in his voice. He hated everything today.

The guy flashed him a sympathetic smile. "There's another airport an hour from here. They have a flight to L.A. leaving in four hours. If you'd like, I can switch your ticket to that airport and get you a rental car for same day return at no extra cost."

Wrecker just wanted to go home. Whatever it took. "Sounds great. Thank you."

Big blue eyes latched on to him. A shy smile touched the guy's lips. "Trust me, I understand wanting to leave this town behind as fast as possible."

Wrecker flashed him a sympathetic smile while trying his best to get the hell out of there. Despite knowing that getting back to L.A. as fast as possible wouldn't change a thing, he still wanted to get home. Coming here with Johnny had been a mistake. Or, hell, maybe it hadn't been. Maybe he needed to see that Johnny came from a wretched family so he could see the real Johnny. Johnny was such a mystery. He was quiet and kept his emotions close to his chest. If Wrecker was being honest, that had been part of the appeal. Wrecker loved a mysterious man. When Johnny looked at Wrecker, his expression never gave anything away, but his eyes were a different story. His eyes burned with silent desire. Wrecker should have known better.

"Here you go, Mr. Lewis. Your new boarding pass and receipt. Just take this over to the rental car area and they'll get you on your way. It was nice meeting you."

Wrecker grabbed his things and nodded. "Thanks, and you too." It was time to get home. Back to the safety of the life he had built for himself. It was time to forget about Johnny. No harm. No foul. Except for Wrecker's broken heart. That didn't matter, though. He had been alone for a long time now. Wrecker was better off that way. He didn't need anyone. Not a single soul. Not even Johnny.

SIX

JOHNNY COULDN'T THINK ABOUT ANYTHING except getting to Wrecker. Wrecker wasn't answering his calls or texts. It had been the longest night in history, with Johnny torn right down the middle. He needed to be with his mom, but he had to fix things with Wrecker. Everything sucked.

When he finally made it back to L.A. and stepped through the door at The Back Porch, all he cared about anymore was getting through to Wrecker. Johnny didn't care if he had to make a scene. Someone clapped, startling him. Before Johnny could figure out what in the hell was going on, someone else joined the first. As Johnny looked on, everyone came to their feet clapping while Johnny stood there lost.

"Congratulations, man," Remington said, patting him on the shoulder.

Johnny nodded, even though he didn't know why. The dark-haired guy was a regular at The Back Porch, but—like everyone there—he never talked to Johnny. The only reason Johnny knew his name at all was because he had been the first one to try flirting with Johnny. "Thanks," Johnny said, sounding confused, even to his ears. "Why?"

A hint of confusion crossed Remington's face. "On the newfound fame, of course. Brett came in here looking for you, and he told everyone the news. As of last night, your video had over a million views and counting. I saw it. You were amazing. Brett says he's been inundated with people begging for more. You're a hit."

A part of Johnny wanted to smile and celebrate. In fact, his lips shaped a smile, but Johnny didn't feel it. "Thanks. That's amazing. Have you seen Wrecker?"

Remington shook his head. "He hasn't been here since early Saturday morning. Theo came in and opened the place this morning."

Johnny nodded and passed along his thanks. He shook hands with a few people. Johnny even managed to stand still so a few people could chat with him. He didn't hear a word anyone said. All Johnny cared about was moving to his next destination, hunting for Wrecker. By the time he disentangled himself and headed toward Wrecker's, he was ready to tear off his skin. Luckily, Wrecker only lived a few streets away. One street over from Ezra's old house. Since he was never home, Johnny hadn't thought to check there first. He didn't know whether to sigh in relief or howl in pain when he saw a car sitting in Wrecker's driveway. It was Brett's car.

Johnny parked beside him and didn't move. As much as he wanted to rush the door and beg Wrecker to listen, he was scared of what he would see. There was no reason for Brett to be here. No good reason anyhow. Brett was successful and beautiful. Johnny wasn't blind. He saw the way Brett always looked at Wrecker. They weren't a couple. Wrecker was free to be with whoever he wanted. In fact, it was entirely possible that Wrecker did have someone he fucked on the regular. Johnny had never asked, but someone as sexy as Wrecker didn't go home alone every night. Johnny wasn't special. They had been trapped in a small bed together. Close proximity had led to intimacy. That was all. He should leave. Wrecker had made it more than clear that Johnny meant nothing. Hell, he hadn't returned a single text since leaving Johnny behind in Illinois. This was dumb.

A knock landed on his window, startling Johnny. Brett stood on the other side, waiting for Johnny to acknowledge him. With his heart in his throat, Johnny rolled down his window.

"I was here looking for you."

At Brett's matter-of-fact statement, Johnny tried swallowing his pain. "My mom had a heart attack and I had to go home for a few days."

Brett nodded, looking sympathetic. "That's what Wrecker just told me. I'm sorry to hear that. After I dropped you off at your truck the other night, I realized I forgot to get your cellphone number. I have a check for you." Brett dug out his wallet and passed him a check from inside. "I don't usually pay people this quickly, since I haven't technically gotten paid from your video yet, but this one time, I wanted you to get a taste of your sudden fame."

Johnny glanced at the check. It was for forty thousand dollars. He blinked. "What's this?"

A bright smile lit Brett's face. "Like I said, it's a small sample of things to come. You're already getting offers from sponsors and people asking you to be their company's ambassador. I know you're here to see Wrecker, but I need your number before I forget again. Also, we need to sit down and make some real plans. We have to strike while you're hot."

Johnny nodded. "Yeah. Of course." He rattled off his number while Brett programmed it into his phone. His gaze slid toward Wrecker's house. Somewhere inside the six-thousand-square-foot home was the man Johnny wanted. His heart screamed for him to get moving. "I've got something to take care of right now, but let's get together later, if you're free."

"Sounds good," Brett said, stuffing his phone back in his pocket. "I have to head over to Jessie's and have a chat with Ezra. If I'm still close by when you get home, shoot me a text. Like I said, let's get a move on. I have so many ideas. You're on your way up."

Johnny tried to smile. He couldn't feel a thing. "I'm ready."

Brett playfully slapped his arm. "I know you are. Now get moving so we can get done what needs to be done."

Johnny nodded and stepped from the truck. He waited until Brett was already in his car and giving Johnny a final wave before heading for Wrecker's door. He rang the doorbell before he could change his mind. When the door swung wide, Johnny's breath caught. There had been this hole inside

Johnny where Wrecker should be, but even Johnny hadn't realized how much he missed Wrecker until he set eyes on him. It didn't even matter that Wrecker didn't look happy to see him. Johnny needed to see Wrecker. He was so royally fucked.

WRECKER'S HEART WAS IN HIS THROAT. WHEN the doorbell rang, he thought it was Brett again since the door had barely closed behind him. Instead, he stared at Johnny. He looked sad and gorgeous. Wrecker immediately wanted to touch him and that pissed him off more than he could say.

"Hi."

Wrecker turned away, leaving the door standing open. If Johnny wanted to stay, he could, but Wrecker wouldn't invite him.

Johnny followed Wrecker through the mud room and into the living room. "I tried to call before I came over, but you didn't answer."

"That should have given you a clue," Wrecker said, hearing the anger in his voice and incapable of stopping it. Damn. Johnny looked ready to bolt. Instead, he shoved his hands in his pockets and visibly swallowed.

"Yeah, I got the hint. You don't want me in your life anymore. Message received." He sounded like he nearly choked on the words. "Give me two minutes, and I'll go. I have something I need to say, and then I'm out."

Wrecker didn't sit and he didn't invite Johnny to either. He shrugged, fighting the urge to scream for Johnny to stay. Instead, his voice remained cold. "Say it, then."

Johnny nodded. "Okay. I'll be quick. When I woke up after our night together, I knew I wanted to be with you. There was nowhere near the confusion in my heart as I expected there to be. The thing is, though, I wasn't prepared to face the immediate hate spewing our way before I even had time to talk to you about what happened between us. I had no plans to hide what I thought we were becoming, but I also needed time to adjust. No one gave me time before jumping in with both feet to rip us to shreds." The more he spoke, the louder Johnny got. It was obvious he was angrier than he let on, but he was trying to control it. "It's unfair as hell that you expect me to just be who you are with no in between or adjustment time." He took an audible breath. Wrecker swore he felt Johnny's frustration, but when he spoke again, he sounded calmer. "I'm sorry,

Wrecker. It was just a lot harder than I expected to be called gay, especially since I don't know what I am. I don't understand anything right now. All I know is, I'm not ready for that label."

"Stop. Just stop," Wrecker said, losing his temper, even though he didn't want that. Johnny had his say. Now it was time for him to hear some truths. "I promised my grandmama on her death bed that I would be real. That I would live my truth and be happy. Do you honestly think I wanted to tank my lifelong dream of playing football so I can open a goddamn coffee shop? I made a choice to live openly. That choice cost me everything. No one will ever say my name again on TV or read my stats without first saying I'm gay. That's all I'll ever be. That gay linebacker. So don't you dare try to tell me how fucking hard it is to be labeled by everyone. I've already paid the price. I won't hide now. Not even for you." The more he spoke, the more he felt Johnny closing against him, and the angrier Wrecker got. "You're the one who said we're not together. So I gave you what you want. We aren't together."

Oddly, Johnny seemed completely calm by the time Wrecker's rant finally finished pouring out. Johnny didn't flinch or look away. He knew his mind. "I wanted you. Exactly as you are," Johnny said, sounding steady. "But you don't want me as I am. I'm sorry that I failed you the first time I was tested. Thank you for being my friend. I'm sorry that I fucked that up." He opened his mouth, as if he had more to say before simply shaking his head and walking away. Johnny left Wrecker behind like he was done. The finality in the air was so complete that Wrecker swore he felt the ties of them sever. As Wrecker stared at the space where Johnny had been only moments earlier, a few truths slowly sank in. Johnny had been trying to save them. That was why he had come here, and Wrecker had been so determined to have his side heard that he hadn't stopped to hear what Johnny had come here to say. He had been so sure he was right that he never considered Johnny might be right too. It wasn't fair for Wrecker to expect him to automatically understand his new role in life. Fuck. If they were both right, then they were both also wrong in some ways, and Wrecker had lost someone who might really love him. His eyes fell closed. He had wanted so badly to force Johnny to see himself for real, Wrecker hadn't considered Johnny's feelings. At some point, being with Johnny had become about being right about the man's sexuality rather than being with someone he loved. Wrecker was pretty freaking positive that Johnny did love him, which meant he had just let the most important person in his life walk away. Goddam it. He had no idea what to do now.

Wrecker headed for the door. They still had things to say. Johnny was right in a lot of ways. Just because he wanted Wrecker didn't necessarily make him gay. There were lots of shades of the rainbow. Wrecker needed to let Johnny figure out where he fit. There was no reason they couldn't do that together. Wrecker opened the door. Johnny was already gone—like he had made a run for it the moment he was out of Wrecker's sight. Wrecker grabbed his phone and tried calling. His call went straight to voicemail. With a growl, he sent a text, asking Johnny to come back and talk. He stared at his phone for five minutes with no response. His heartbeat pounded in his ears. Since the moment he left Johnny behind, the rage had been building. The images of Johnny pulling and tugging, fighting to be closer to Wrecker kept invading his mind. He couldn't stop seeing Johnny's face—the desperation— as he practically begged to suck Wrecker's dick. No one had ever been that way with him. There had never been anyone like Johnny in Wrecker's life and Wrecker was too big of a mess to see he was the one standing in their way. He was the one who hated being the gay. The roar inside his mind grew and built until Wrecker threw his phone against the wall. It shattered as it punched a hole in the wall. Wrecker's chest heaved like he had been running for miles. Just like everything in his life, Wrecker didn't know how to make this right. They were just done, and he was alone again.

SEVEN

IT WAS FUNNY HOW MUCH NOTHING MATTERED any more. Brett had come through for Johnny and then some. Five days after his video uploaded on his new channel, while Johnny had still been grieving the loss of Wrecker, his video had gone viral. One song and video had made him more money in a week than he had ever made at one time in his life. Once upon a time, Johnny would have given his left nut to find the fame that had found him while he wasn't even looking. Now, here he was nonstop practicing a song that Jessie Thunder had written and getting ready to perform it online for hundreds of thousands of subscribers. That was unreal to him. Yet he wasn't the least bit happy. Not even the tiniest bit.

"Don't get me wrong, I'm not interested in

touring again. Not at all. But it is pretty exciting to be working again." Johnny smiled while Jessie talked a mile a minute. His cheeks ached from faking it. "I mean, I wish YouTube had been the way to fame back in my day, because this is way less stressful. Plus, like, there's the whole drug usage side of things. It's a lot easier to stay sober and grounded while performing from home with my husband at my side. This is awesome."

Johnny nodded, trying to keep up, even as his throat kept swelling unexpectedly every five seconds. "It's definitely awesome." Johnny didn't have to say much to keep Jessie talking while he wallowed in his misery.

"I still can't believe that you've been working with me for years and you never once talked to me about your dreams. We're friends. I would've introduced you to anyone and everyone to help make you famous."

Johnny shrugged. He loved Jessie. Jessie had a heart of gold. "You're my friend. That's worth more to me than being famous."

A bright smile lit Jessie's face. He was such a brightly burning star. Even if Johnny didn't know Jessie was famous, he would still know it. He was blinding. "We can still be friends while I help your career. I know you're not the type to use people. Hell, you took a drink to the chest for me the first time we met. You're a naturally selfless person. You deserve to be treated the same."

Johnny swallowed. He fought against the wave of loss that kept trying to suck him under. He was drowning and no one noticed. For the love of all things holy, he could not keep talking about himself. He wasn't the least bit selfless. All anyone had to do was ask Wrecker. He would tell them the truth. "Theo will be blown away by this song you've written for him. I can't wait to see his face."

Theo was always the right topic to distract Jessie. Jessie was blindingly in love with his husband. It was adorable. "Dude, it has been murder trying to keep this hidden from him. Well, you know me, I'm not the secretive type. I already tell my every thought. He knows something is up, because I usually tell him everything that I'm doing every second of the day. It'll be worth it, though. I love surprising him."

Ezra slipped into the room, making sure he didn't let Icarus slide inside behind him. The dog he shared with his husband Declan followed Ezra everywhere. Once they were alone, Ezra looked his way with a bright smile. "Hey. Are you getting excited? Nervous? How are you feeling?"

Johnny fought the urge to say the first thing to come to mind. He felt completely alone in the world. This didn't feel like his life. Johnny sort of wanted to just get up, walk away now, and forget the last nine years in L.A. Maybe he would.

"I'm good," he lied. After all, it seemed he had been lying his entire life.

Ezra eyed him—like he saw beneath Johnny's mask. He chewed his bottom lip, making Johnny wonder what he saw. "You do seem extremely subdued, even for you."

Johnny smiled. He didn't feel it, but that didn't matter. He couldn't stop. "I know. I'm boring."

"You're still waters," Ezra said, pulling a chair close to Johnny. "Brett will be here any minute, so be honest with me. How are you feeling about all this?"

He searched for a plausible lie before Ezra's genuine concern beat him down. The door flew open, saving him. Brett swept in like the hurricane he was, capturing all the attention. Johnny became just another grain of sand swept along in the tidal wave of Brett's trip to the top of everything he touched. Johnny seemed to be the only one who recognized that truth. Brett was the real star. Everyone else was just hanging on for the ride.

Brett barely spared anyone a glance. "This is

what we're going to do," Brett said, talking with his hands—like he was in business mode. "Since Ezra has a crazy popular channel, he'll interview you before your performance. I'll upload the interview to your channel and his, hitting both fan bases. I think, between those two things and Jessie being here, everyone will know your name by the end of the week."

Johnny nodded. His didn't feel a damn thing, even though he was among friends and his dreams were blooming around him. The most important friend he had was missing. Johnny felt that empty spot all the way to his bones, but the world kept turning. In a matter of minutes, he found his guitar dragged to one side of him while Ezra sat facing him. Ezra looked poised with his pink highlights on point and his features flawless, as always. Brett handed him notes and Ezra flashed Johnny a smile.

"You've got this."

Johnny nodded, even though he was fairly certain he did not in fact have this. That doubt didn't stop it from happening. Theo and Declan appeared in the doorway to watch. Brett held up three fingers and silently counted them down.

Ezra smiled at the camera, transforming into the star he was online. "Hey, guys. I have a special treat for you today. Recently, a new and rare talent hit the scene, taking the world by storm with his amazing voice. Somehow, I managed to snag him for a quick interview and private performance. Everyone, welcome Johnny Savage."

Johnny dipped his chin at the camera before fixating on Ezra. "Hey, Ra. Thanks for the invite."

Ezra winked. "Thank you for taking time out of your busy schedule to let me ask you a few questions. The world is dying to get to know you."

Even though it was Ezra, and they had been friends for years, Johnny fought a blush. "I'm happy to be here." He didn't know what else to say since he hadn't expected an interview.

Ezra's professionalism didn't waver. "Since I know your time is precious, let's jump right in. Someone told me that you moved to L.A. the day after you turned eighteen. Even though I know that's not a terribly uncommon thing and a lot of people come here hoping to make it, I would love to know more. It's been nine years. What happened when you got here?"

Without thought, Johnny chuckled. "Well, honestly, when I got here, I immediately realized I wouldn't be taking anything by storm like I expected. Obviously, I had a lot of confidence in my abilities to take the risk, but I really had no idea. Everyone here is beautiful and talented. I quickly realized there was nothing special about me at all. Plus, I don't really like hiking, so I didn't fit in," he added with a laugh.

Ezra chuckled along. "We do love our hiking trails. Still, though, you definitely had iron nerves on your side, leaving home at just eighteen to come all the way across the country to follow a dream."

Johnny nodded. "You know, I used to think about how I jumped in my truck and drove across the country with a thousand dollars to my name, and I would be like—that's the craziest slash dumbest slash bravest shit imaginable. Like, nowadays, I'm blown away I was that ballsy. Then I met my best friend and learned I didn't know anything about being brave. He's shown me what real courage looks like, and that maybe I don't have as much of it as I would like to think." Johnny's throat swelled on the confession.

"Would you like to give a shout out to your best friend while I have you here?"

Johnny shook his head, fighting to regain his voice. "As I learned from recently attending a hockey game with him, he doesn't really like it when the spotlight falls on him. So I won't do that." Plus, they weren't friends anymore.

Ezra smacked his knee with the script of questions he held. "Well, I think you're scary talented. Dumb or crazy, your risk paid off in a big way. You're now sitting in Jessie Thunder's personal recording studio, and you'll soon be singing a brand new, never-heard-before song written by Jessie Thunder himself for his new husband. Topping off that amazingness, Jessie will also be accompanying you on drums." Brett swung the camera Jessie's way. Jessie nodded and twirled his sticks, patiently waiting to get started. The camera came back to rest on Ezra and Johnny. Ezra stayed completely professional. "Are you ready to get started? I know Jessie's husband Theo has been dying to know what's going on."

Johnny nodded, hoping he didn't fuck this up after everything Jessie had done for him. The camera zoomed in on him and Johnny picked up his guitar. Jessie counted out the beat and Johnny joined in, strumming a few chords before falling into the music. He sang, forgetting everyone else was there. Nothing existed but the words and rhythm. He went to a place he loved inside himself. The music became his new world. When it ended, he snapped back to reality, blinking at his surroundings as he realized he wasn't alone. Theo had his hand covering his mouth.

His eyes swam with tears. As he looked on, Jessie crossed the room and pulled Theo into his arms. He spoke in quiet tones, telling Theo how much he loved him, and praising him for saving him when the drugs were winning. Johnny's throat swelled. He realized something massive. He had taken Theo on a journey of Jessie's love. Johnny had given life to Jessie's song and painted an image that held a magnifying glass to Jessie's emotions for Theo to see. He had done that. It was humbling and scarily addictive. Johnny already wanted to do it again. There was just one thing, though. Wrecker wasn't there to share the moment with him, and that devastated him on a level he couldn't describe.

"That was Johnny Savage, singing 'You Found Me in an Ocean.' If you would like to see Johnny and Jessie perform this new single live, you can purchase tickets in the link down below. Don't forget to hit that like button and subscribe. Until next time, this is Ra Lee signing out."

Brett made a slashing motion, signaling they were wrapped. Johnny pasted on a faked smile and accepted all the hugs. Jessie and Theo had already disappeared inside their room. Ezra was on the way out too, ready to be alone with Declan. Brett said something about needing to do edits and get the show uploaded. In a matter of minutes, Johnny was alone again. His adrenaline rush faded. It was just him and nothing else. The way things always were. It was time for him to accept that would never change. Wrecker had only been a dream.

Before Johnny could convince himself to leave, the studio door opened again. Brett stepped back inside.

"I thought you left."

Brett smiled at the comment and moved farther into the room. "I almost did, but then I got in the car, and I couldn't leave yet."

In his confusion, Johnny chuckled. "Okay. Is everything all right?"

"You tell me," Brett said, claiming the chair Ezra used in the interview. His blue gaze held Johnny's, making him feel like he could see all the way to his soul. The professional was gone. For the first time, Johnny felt like he stared at the real version of Brett. This wasn't the star. It wasn't the eccentric genius. Johnny saw the person beneath all that. Still, he didn't know what Brett expected to hear.

"I don't know what you're digging for right now."

Brett chewed his bottom lip, drawing Johnny's gaze to his mouth. The man really was too pretty to be a man. His features were flawless. Brett took an audible breath—like bracing himself. "Did Wrecker and you break up?"

Johnny blinked. "I'm sorry. What?"

Brett sat straighter, visibly squaring his shoulders. Johnny found himself needing to know what the guy would say next. "I've known Wrecker for years—for a lot longer than anyone else in this town. We met back when he played football for Georgia and I'd like to think I know him better than most. He doesn't have friends."

Johnny opened his mouth to argue. After all, if nothing else, Ezra was Wrecker's friend.

Brett's hand slashed through the air before Johnny could say as much. "He has people he likes, people who help him out at The Back Porch, and people he'll sit with there and visit. But Wrecker doesn't have real friends. So the fact that he took you to a hockey game and closed his coffeehouse when your mom had a heart attack, that says something. It says a lot of somethings. Yet he's not here today and you look ready to fall apart at the slightest wrong word, so what happened?"

"Wrecker closed the coffeehouse? He told me he had an employee he trusted to run the place while we were gone."

Brett shook his head. "He doesn't trust anyone

that much, except Ezra or Theo maybe, but that's a lot to ask Ezra right now, and Jessie isn't exactly letting Theo out of his sight. So Wrecker closed the place for a few days."

Johnny blinked. He couldn't even fathom that. That meant Johnny really needed to be honest about them. When Johnny had gone to Wrecker's to apologize, he had been serious when he said he had wanted to be with Wrecker. Wrecker hadn't wanted that too, but Johnny had meant every word. To that point, he needed to mean that claim even when Wrecker didn't want him anymore. "As you said, we broke up."

The way Brett blinked said way more than Johnny imagined he wanted. Brett had been taking a stab in the dark. He hadn't one hundred percent believed Johnny had been with Wrecker as more than friends. Brett cleared his throat. "You still called him your best friend during the interview."

Johnny shrugged. "He is. Maybe he doesn't want me or that title anymore, but his desires don't change my feelings. Until I stop feeling it, he's still my best friend." Johnny blinked at the sudden lump in his throat. "And I get that I'll eventually have to stop feeling it."

A flash of pain crossed Brett's features and

Johnny saw the man's heart. "I'm sorry. He told me you were straight, so I didn't warn you about him. Wrecker is gorgeous and successful and caring and sweet. He's everything everyone is looking for in a man. Unfortunately, at the end of the day, Wrecker is also stubborn and unbending and forever changed by what he's lost. Football was the one and only thing he's ever loved in this world and he lost it because of something he can't change about himself. Wrecker chose to double-down and open a business that acts as a haven for gay men—like a fuck you to all the haters. But I'm not sure he's ever stopped hating that part of himself. No one else really stands a chance."

Johnny thought about Wrecker's expression while Johnny's grandfather had been spewing hate. Jenny had tried standing up for him, but he had felt Wrecker closing off from the world. That was the real reason he had started to panic. While he had always been extra sensitive to yelling, it was Wrecker's vibe that choked him. He had felt Wrecker pulling away and Johnny had broken. Brett was right. Johnny had never stood a chance. "It's okay."

Johnny heard the words fall from his lips, but they felt like they came from a long way off—like someone else had said them. He didn't feel okay at all. "Being with Wrecker was always temporary, I think. He was like a... I don't know. A passing dream, I guess. You know, kind of like when the most popular guy in school sits next to you, because there's nowhere else left to sit on the bus. Instead of ignoring you, like you expect, he talks to you the entire ride like you're the best of friends, but the whole time you know once you leave that bus, he'll never speak to you again. That's what it's like loving Wrecker. He's not intentionally cruel. He just doesn't realize that his kindness kills people when he takes it away."

Brett's lips parted in surprise.

Johnny stood. "Thank you for checking on me. I know you're super busy and every second you take away from work is a second you're falling behind. So I really do appreciate you. Don't worry about me, though. I'm used to sitting alone on the bus." Johnny walked away, setting Brett free. They both had things to do, and the sooner Johnny got started, the faster he could disappear.

BRETT: *I FELT MOVED TO TELL YOU THAT YOU'RE*

an asshole. You're a nice person, so I don't think anyone has ever truly told you that. You need to hear it, though. Other people matter too. Not just you... Asshole.

All that was true, so Wrecker didn't bother answering Brett's text. It wasn't like they had anything to say to each other. Wrecker had work to do. If he was being honest with himself, he couldn't believe it had taken Brett this long to send him a text, calling Wrecker out of his name.

Ezra: *Johnny has a new video up on YouTube. You have to see it. He was SO good. You'll die.*

While Wrecker also didn't answer Ezra's text when it came in, he hadn't stopped thinking about it all night. Johnny hadn't been to The Back Porch since walking away from Wrecker almost two weeks ago. Wrecker had been busy with work. He kept hoping Johnny would come back to the coffee shop and go back to low-key flirting with Wrecker. In fact, Wrecker would give just about anything to go back to those days when Johnny was still his friend. He wanted Johnny in his life in whatever capacity he could have him. Wrecker knew exactly when he had gone too far, expected too much. He had always been a loner, but now he felt the silence in his life like a physical touch.

While sitting alone in his empty and closed coffeehouse, Wrecker opened his YouTube app. He searched for Johnny's channel and pulled up the new video. A smile pulled at the corners of his mouth as Ezra appeared on the screen. It was just like Ezra to try his damnedest to mold his friends into the happy vision he had of their lives. Wrecker leaned his phone against a sugar shaker and rested his chin on his crossed arms. He leaned as close as he could to the screen, settling in to watch.

Ezra smiled. "Hey, guys. I have a special treat for you today. Recently, a new and rare talent hit the scene, taking the world by storm with his amazing voice. Somehow, I managed to snag him for a quick interview and private performance. Everyone, welcome Johnny Savage."

Johnny appeared on the screen. Wrecker took a breath. His eyes were sad. Even as he returned Ezra's smile, he looked unhappy as hell. "Hey, Ra. Thanks for the invite."

Ezra winked, looking completely oblivious to Johnny's misery. "Thank you for taking time out of your busy schedule to let me ask you a few questions. The world is dying to get to know you."

"I'm happy to be here." Goddamn. No, he

wasn't. Wrecker couldn't breathe. Why did no one else see that Johnny was drowning?

"Since I know your time is precious, let's jump right in. Someone told me that you moved to L.A. the day after you turned eighteen. Even though I know that's not a terribly uncommon thing and a lot of people come here hoping to make it, I would love to know more. It's been nine years. What happened when you got here?"

Johnny chuckled. The tension in Wrecker's chest eased a hair. "Well, honestly, when I got here, I immediately realized I wouldn't be taking anything by storm like I expected. Obviously, I had a lot of confidence in my abilities to take that risk, but I really had no idea. Everyone here is beautiful and talented. I quickly realized there was nothing special about me at all. Plus, I don't really like hiking, so I didn't fit in," he added with a laugh.

Ezra chuckled. "We do love our hiking trails. Still, though, you definitely had iron nerves on your side, leaving home at just eighteen to come all the way across the country to follow a dream."

Johnny nodded. "You know, I used to think about how I jumped in my truck and drove across the country with a thousand dollars to my name, and I would be like—that's the craziest slash dumbest slash bravest shit imaginable. Like, nowadays, I'm blown away I was that ballsy. Then I met my best friend and learned I didn't know anything about being brave. He's shown me what real courage looks like, and that maybe I don't have as much of it as I would like to think."

Wrecker couldn't fucking breathe.

"Would you like to give a shout out to your best friend while I have you here?"

Johnny shook his head. He looked like he choked on his unhappiness. "As I learned from recently attending a hockey game with him, he doesn't really like it when the spotlight falls on him. So I won't do that."

Wrecker didn't hear another word. Johnny thought Wrecker was brave. He wasn't. Not at all. Wrecker was the biggest fucking coward on the planet. He could have gone to Johnny any time in the past two weeks and worked things out. Instead, he had been waiting for Johnny to come to him. Just as he had expected Johnny to accept dating a man publicly at the snap of his fingers. Wrecker couldn't stop being the one who expected Johnny to do all the bending. It was no wonder Johnny looked ready to break.

Wrecker flew to his feet, grabbed his phone, and

headed out. The fifteen-minute drive to Jessie's place felt like a goddamn eternity. No one tried stopping him after he punched the code in at the gate. As he parked outside the garage, he expected Johnny to appear. He didn't. There were too many cars in Jessie's darkened garage to tell if Johnny's truck was one of them, so Wrecker jogged up the spiral staircase to Johnny's loft. The door stood open and the lights were off. Wrecker tapped his knuckles on the door as he stepped inside.

"Hello. It's Wrecker. Don't shoot or anything."

Silence met his words. He stepped farther into the room. The place felt empty. The covers were missing from the bed and the bookshelves were empty. Wrecker turned in a slow circle. The loft looked exactly like a fully furnished apartment before anyone moved in. He headed for the closet. Before Wrecker opened the door, he knew what he would find. It was empty. Johnny was gone.

"He left yesterday after recording his latest video."

Wrecker spun.

Declan stood in the doorway.

"Where did he go?"

Declan shrugged. "He packed up his truck and left."

Wrecker moved to the couch and sat. He hated that his legs stopped working in front of Declan, considering how much Declan hated him, but Wrecker had been so set to do whatever it took to get Johnny back, and he was gone. Wrecker didn't know what to do now.

Declan crossed the room and joined him on the couch. "You have that look about you. What did you do to run him off?"

As much as Wrecker wanted to roll his eyes at the question, he couldn't. It felt a hell of a lot like his fault. "I refused to let him keep pretending he's straight."

Declan drew back. "Johnny is straight?"

A snort escaped Wrecker. "He seemed to think so until we ended up in bed together. You didn't know?"

For a moment, Declan stared into space before focusing on Wrecker again. "I know that it's kind of the go-to to think that everyone is straight unless they say otherwise, but Johnny has worked here for nine years. I guess I just assumed that he was like everyone here."

Wrecker's forehead furrowed. "But surely in nine years you saw him bring people home or whatever."

Declan shook his head. "I worked days and Johnny worked nights, but still, no. Johnny didn't bring people home. He was kind of always alone. Sometimes, I worried about him, but he seemed happy enough. Then he started hanging out with you and I just assumed you two were together, or whatever."

Wrecker stared at nothing and turned Declan's words over in his head. What the hell was Johnny's story? Why hadn't Wrecker asked more questions?

"Do you remember the first time someone called you gay?" Declan's question pulled him from his spiraling thoughts.

Wrecker wracked his brain. "Not really."

Declan surprised him. "I do. I was twelve and already two feet taller and fifty pounds heavier than everyone in my class. Obviously, I made that little prick regret it, but I can remember exactly how I lost my breath. I felt like I had fallen from a tree and had the air knocked out of me. It wasn't a lie. Yeah, the kid had only been calling me gay as a childish taunt. No one really knew that about me back then, but I knew."

Wrecker got what Declan was trying to say. "I don't remember the first time anyone said it, but I do remember turning on the TV the day after I came out publicly. For the first time in my life, I was on every channel and it had nothing to do with my football career. I scrolled through my phone and it was every headline. My Facebook and Twitter were filled with private messages. Bible verses. Death threats. I remember the first time I walked into the locker room afterward." Wrecker stopped. He couldn't tell anyone the way it felt to have people he had considered his family hide their nudity like he would fall on them—like a rapist.

Declan stood, dragging Wrecker from the sensation of drowning. "No matter how accepting the people are surrounding you, everyone has to go through that moment. Everyone handles it differently."

And Wrecker had made that moment a million times worse for Johnny. Wrecker swallowed. "I need to find him."

With a sigh, Declan pulled his phone from his back pocket and spent a moment typing. The device buzzed, sounding loud in the otherwise silent room. "He's at the Casita Bungalows in Santa Barbara. Cabin fifteen. I told him I had to send him some shit from Jessie."

Santa Barbara was only about a hundred miles away. Wrecker could be there in no time. He flew to his feet. "Thank you. I know you don't really like me, so I hope you know how much I appreciate this."

Declan cocked his head to one side and eyed Wrecker. "I never said I don't like you."

A smile exploded across Wrecker's face. "You didn't have to say it."

To his surprise, Declan shook his head. "No. Really. I always assumed you hated me, so I've just steered clear of you. Ezra loves you and I love him, so I have nothing against you."

"I thought you were crazy. Before you married Ezra," Wrecker explained. "I used to see you sitting outside his house late at night and I worried."

A bright smile lit Declan's face. "I am crazy. Loving Ezra has made me this way." Declan shrugged. "I'm not ashamed. There's no such thing as shame in love. If you're ashamed of how far you'll go for someone you love, you don't really love them. I love Ezra. If he ever tried to leave me, I would follow him everywhere, serenading him every step. He would take me back just to get some peace. I wouldn't stop."

Wrecker couldn't stop smiling at the image Declan painted, and he kind of got it. Johnny was about to regret running away from him. Wrecker had no plans of stopping now that he realized how much he had lost. There had been nothing he could do when he lost his football career. Johnny wasn't the same. Wrecker could and would do anything it took to get him back. Wrecker was about to show him what crazy looked like.

EIGHT

A WARM BREEZE RUFFLED JOHNNY'S HAIR AS HE tipped his head back and drained the last few inches of beer from his bottle. He set the empty bottle aside and grabbed another. He twisted off the cap and set the porch swing back into motion. Johnny had a solid plan to achieve peace come hell or high water. Either the sound of the ocean and the night air would set him at ease, or a drunken oblivion would carry him away. Either way, Johnny wouldn't spend another night thinking about Wrecker. If blacking out was what it took, so be it. This was his new life.

One hundred miles away from the man he loved, and the life he lived for the past nine years, Johnny planned to start over. This bungalow was only the beginning. He had been saving almost every dime he made for the past nine years and he had made a shit ton of money in a very short period with Brett's help. This little getaway on the beach was only a temporary stopping point while Johnny plotted his next move. He had to get away to think clearly. Being surrounded by a house filled with people in love was too hard right now. He had committed to one live venue event for Brett. Beyond that, Johnny didn't know what he wanted. For a long time, he had been content with his lot in life. Things had been peaceful and quiet. Johnny missed the peace.

"I wish you knew how many times I watched you when you weren't looking. You never get less gorgeous to me."

Johnny froze with his beer halfway to his mouth. For a moment, he couldn't turn his head. He had never been more certain he was hallucinating. His gaze slowly slid to the right. Wrecker stood, looking unsure of his welcome. "Why are you here?"

Wrecker moved a few steps closer. "Because you are."

Johnny went back to staring at the ocean. "I have beer, if you're thirsty."

"I see that," Wrecker said, moving closer. "I also see you've been partaking for a hot minute."

Maybe there was a myriad of empty bottles next

to the cooler. Johnny hadn't been counting. He shrugged. "I have nowhere to be." Johnny scooted over so Wrecker could join him on the swing. He passed Wrecker a beer and together they set the swing back in motion.

For a long minute, they sat in companionable silence before Wrecker broke it. "I lied when I said I don't know my parents," Wrecker said while staring at the ocean. Johnny couldn't tear his eyes away from Wrecker. He was gorgeous and Johnny had missed his face. "They were terrible people who wanted nothing to do with me until I got rich, that is," Wrecker said, flashing Johnny a bitter-looking smile. "Then they were doing TV interviews and lying about how proud they were and how Dad had been practicing with me every day growing up, because he knew I would be a star. I didn't even know that bastard's name until I saw him on TV, talking about how much he did for me. When everything fell apart, they tried to sue me for ruining their lives by choosing the gay lifestyle. When your grandfather accused me of doing the same thing to you, dragging you down with me, it struck a nerve, I guess." Wrecker drank half his beer while Johnny kept watching. Finally, Wrecker looked Johnny's way again. "I'm sorry."

Johnny couldn't stop staring at him, even though it hurt his chest. He had never missed anyone or anything as much as he had missed Wrecker. Looking at him soothed something inside Johnny that nothing else touched. "You have nothing to be sorry about."

A sad smile touched Wrecker's lips. "That's not true at all. You have every right to take your time and figure out where you fall in this whole spectrum thing. I had no right to rush you or label you or expect you to be what I want. When I left your mom's place, it didn't have anything to do with you, as it turns out. You deserved better from me. I could see that you were drowning, and I was a shit friend."

Johnny nodded, accepting Wrecker's apology, even though he wasn't sure who was right or if anyone was wrong. He draped his arm across the back of the swing, giving Wrecker more room. Plus, he liked Wrecker's warmth and it made Johnny feel like he held him. "I don't handle it well when people yell. My dad was always angry, yelling, and throwing things. I have his temper, but I also kind of freeze when people start getting loud. Grandpa and Jenny were in their screaming match and he was being awful, because he's always awful, and I just wanted it to stop before it ruined us, and then I destroyed us." Johnny shook his head. "I don't blame you for leaving. Hell, I wanted to leave too."

"You're my best friend," Wrecker said, sounding earnest—like he needed Johnny to believe him. "I should've stayed or swept you away from that mess. That's on me." He leaned Johnny's way a hair. Maybe no one else would have noticed, but Johnny always saw every slight movement Wrecker made. Wrecker finished his beer and set the empty bottle aside before meeting Johnny's stare again. "What are you doing here anyhow? All your things were gone from the loft."

"I'm finding myself."

A sexy rumble of laughter vibrated from Wrecker. "By sitting on a porch swing and drinking?"

A smile exploded across Johnny's face. He was so goddamn happy to be with Wrecker. The hows or whys of the situation didn't matter. Johnny just loved being in Wrecker's company. "Drinking is a huge part of the finding myself experience. I also bought a bunch of sex toys and I'm figuring out what I like."

Wrecker shook his head. His smile never slipped. "You have no idea how fast you get me hard. Like, you didn't even blush confessing that, and my body was immediately like goddamn, let's go then. For real, you turn me on. Does anything embarrass you?"

Johnny shrugged. "I guess I'm not the blushing type. Plus, I'm drunk as hell. Didn't you wade through the forest of empty beer bottles to sit with me?" Johnny couldn't stop smiling. Being with Wrecker was like popping happy pills. Johnny never wanted it to stop.

"I love you." Johnny's smile slipped away. Shock replaced everything. Wrecker didn't stop to give him time to think. "It's only fair for me to be one hundred percent real with you. I'm in love with you. Like I said, you're my best friend, but I want more. I want to be with you—like a real couple. If you don't want that, or if you need me to give you time, that's cool. I will, but I also need you to know where I stand. You're who I want. I am completely in love with you."

It turned out, Johnny didn't need to think. He just needed to hear Wrecker say exactly what he said. Johnny slid his hand across Wrecker's shoulders until he cupped his nape. He drew Wrecker closer. "I love you too." He met Wrecker halfway. Their lips brushed. "You're who I want."

At his confession, Wrecker buried his fingers in Johnny's hair. He tugged and held Johnny in place as he deepened their kiss. "Tell me about these toys. I want to hear more," Wrecker said as he changed angles, but then he immediately deepened their kiss again so Johnny couldn't answer. Wrecker pulled away again. "Let's go inside and make out."

Johnny stood, pulling Wrecker to his feet as he went. He didn't need to hear the suggestion twice. Wrecker was here. They were okay. Everything else could wait. Right now, Johnny just wanted to fucking hold the man who had stolen him when he wasn't looking. He wanted to be with Wrecker.

As Johnny led Wrecker inside, Wrecker cast a cursory glance at the place. It looked the way a small bungalow usually looked. Small kitchen. Big bed. Uncomfortably hard couch. Wrecker didn't care about anything but the bed. Johnny wasn't wearing a shirt and his shorts hugged his ass. He had talked about experimenting with toys the same way he had spoken right before sucking Wrecker's dick—zero shame. Wrecker hadn't been lying. He had gone hard at the first mention of toys and he was aching for Johnny. It was like he needed to stake his claim now before Johnny changed his mind.

Johnny had said he loved Wrecker. Wrecker hadn't expected that. Of course, he also hadn't planned to say those words himself. Then, the moment he set eyes on Johnny, Wrecker had been lost. He loved Johnny. It would have been a disservice to them both to stay quiet, so he hadn't. Now he wanted Johnny's body beneath him. He overcame Johnny before he reached the bed, pulling the man back against his chest. His hand automatically dropped to Johnny's crotch. When he found Johnny hard, the last brain cell Wrecker possessed went into hiding. He had met a lot of people over the years. This one belonged to him. Wrecker wanted to do lots of dirty things to him.

"I'm your toy now. Your own personal sex doll." He bit the side of Johnny's neck. "There's nothing I won't do, except accept another person in our bed. I don't share, and I'm freaky enough to keep you entertained by myself."

Johnny shoved his hand between them and massaged Wrecker's hard cock through his jeans. "Good. I want you to fuck me."

Wrecker swore his body jerked—like Johnny short-circuited him. He never expected that demand. "Are you sure?" Even Wrecker heard the question in his voice. He genuinely expected Johnny to take it back.

Johnny put his hand over Wrecker's and led it to his dick. He rubbed while writhing against Wrecker's body, grinding his ass against Wrecker's erection. "Don't you feel how much I want it?"

If Johnny wanted to get fucked, Wrecker was his man. He went to work, stripping Johnny before tearing off his own clothes. He couldn't toss the material away fast enough to suit his heart. Wrecker needed to be inside Johnny, claiming him. "Tell me how you see this in your head." Johnny's forehead furrowed and Wrecker tried clarifying. "Are you looking up at me or straddling my body? Do you want to bury your face in the mattress and let me have my way?" He moved close and hauled Johnny against him, so their erections bumped. Wrecker smoothed his hand over the curve of Johnny's bare ass. "Are you on your side while I take you gently from behind? How do you see this?"

"I want to look in your eyes."

Wrecker's throat suddenly swelled. Johnny made him proud. He was so goddamn brave. There had been a huge part of Wrecker that believed they were done. He had just known in his heart that Johnny wouldn't fuck with him anymore. Yet, here he was, asking Wrecker to look him in the eyes when he made love to him. He made Wrecker a mess. "I can do that." Wrecker walked him backward toward the bed. At the edge of the mattress, he pushed, sending Johnny tumbling. He stared down at the man who had stolen his heart and craved for Johnny to take more. "Where's the lube?"

Johnny motioned toward a small bag sitting in a hardback chair nearby. "In that bag."

Wrecker stooped and grabbed his jeans from the floor. He dug his only condom from his wallet before heading for the bag. When he looked inside, pre-cum rolled down his length. Johnny hadn't been lying. He had toys. Wrecker wanted to watch Johnny trying every single one, but he only had the one condom. Right now, it was all about the lube. He found the bottle and carried it back to the bed. Johnny's heated gaze followed his every move while his hard cock leaked on his stomach. Wrecker stood over him while he rolled the condom down his length.

"I had a talk with Declan before I came here." Wrecker climbed on the bed and kissed Johnny's chest. "He said he had never seen you bring anyone home." He squirted a crazy amount of lube in his hand. Johnny's thighs parted—like he had zero doubts. Wrecker kept talking while he played, fingering Johnny. Stretching. Lubing his hole. "His comment had me thinking all the way here." Wrecker shifted positions and settled between Johnny's legs. He pushed Johnny's knees higher, making room. Wrecker stroked Johnny's dick, trying to keep him distracted. "Declan said y'all worked different shifts, so it wasn't surprising he had never actually seen you bring anyone home, but still, I'm not so sure." Wrecker worked his fingers inside Johnny, massaging his prostate.

Johnny panted and grasped at the sheets. Still, his gaze stayed locked on Wrecker's face. He never looked away. "You're so fucking sexy. Your eyes haunt me."

Wrecker smirked. "You know how to use your words to stroke me, but I can't be distracted right now. Because, you see, I know I'm the first man who's getting up in this sexy ass." To prove his point, Wrecker rubbed Johnny's asshole with his crown. He pushed his way in a hair and then retreated. "But now, after talking to Declan." Wrecker pushed his way in again. This time, he only dipped inside about an inch before retreating. He held Johnny's stare. His body rocked forward, sliding in. Johnny was so tight. Wrecker unconsciously stroked Johnny's dick, trying to ease the pain of being stretched. Johnny bit his bottom lip while white-knuckling the sheets. Still, he held Wrecker's stare. Sweat beaded on Wrecker's skin as he finally got all the way inside. He stayed still, letting Johnny adjust. His heart couldn't take it. He was with the one person he loved. Wrecker leaned in and claimed Johnny's mouth. He rocked without thrusting, needing Johnny to feel good too. Wrecker stroked Johnny, jacking him off. He lost his train of thought with his dick buried inside Johnny.

"Goddamn, Johnny. I want to watch you fuck that flesh light you brought and that silicon ass. Jesus. I want you to fuck those things while I bury my dick in your ass and pound. You make me hot as hell. I don't want to hurt you, but I promise it'll feel good soon." That was all the warning Wrecker gave before he snaked his arms beneath Johnny's knees, pulling them higher, and thrust. He made sure he hit at the right angle because he needed Johnny to feel good, but he couldn't wait any longer. Johnny was too tight and hot. His body was trying to suck Wrecker deeper and steal his orgasm. Wrecker needed to make Johnny come first. He kept up the dirty talk as the ecstasy built. "Your asshole feels so good, Johnny. I want to stay here all night. You belong to me. I'll make you moan and laugh. Goddamn. I can't stop my mouth from watering. It knows how you taste. I want to suck your dick, but I can't give up this ass yet."

Johnny grabbed his cock and stroked—like he couldn't take the torment any longer.

Wrecker couldn't breathe properly at the sight of Johnny pleasuring himself. "That's it, sexy. Torture me. I like to watch."

"Fuck," Johnny growled, fucking his fist. "You feel good, Wrecker. Don't stop. Shit. I'm going to come." Johnny's body tensed. His asshole tightened around Wrecker's cock. The muscles in Johnny's neck strained as he pumped faster on his dick. Wrecker held his breath. His eyes burned from refusing to blink against the sight. A loud pant burst from Johnny and then lights exploded behind Wrecker's eyes as Johnny's body sucked hard, jerking an orgasm from Wrecker before he was ready. He gasped, riding out the waves. Wrecker couldn't stop rocking his hips, seeking more. He fell on Johnny, sucking his tongue and biting his lips. His mind was all over the place, but his heart was steady. This was the one for him. Wrecker would never give him up. He finally understood why Declan behaved so crazy when it came to Ezra. Wrecker felt pretty fucking crazed too. No one would take Johnny from him. He would kill anyone who tried. Wrecker had never felt so primal—like he fought for his soul. They were meant to be. He felt it in his bones. No one would come between them.

Johnny couldn't stop toying with Wrecker's hand. It felt so good in his arms and a happy buzz rang in his head. Johnny was a sun child. He was dark blond and tanned dark. His hand didn't look all that pale against Wrecker's darker skin. Johnny filed that detail away with the million other tiny details he had gathered about Wrecker since they had met. He wanted to hear all Wrecker's stories, but he also wanted to tell Wrecker everything about his life. Forever didn't feel like long enough to say everything.

"I wasn't a virgin."

Wrecker chuckled. The sound vibrated against Johnny's ear that was pressed to Wrecker's chest. The sound made him smile. "What?"

"I thought that was what you were getting at earlier. When you talked about your conversation with Declan," Johnny clarified. "I thought you were leading up to saying you wondered if I had ever been with anyone else."

Wrecker stroked his hair. "You blew my mind and I forgot, but yeah, that's what I wondered after talking to Declan."

Johnny's smile grew. He loved talking to Wrecker, because he loved seeing Wrecker react to his every story. That was why Johnny couldn't stop talking now. "When I was seventeen, there was this girl that I wanted more than I wanted my next breath. All my friends thought I was crazy because she wasn't what most guys were after. She wasn't classically pretty. Plus, she was abrasive as hell and gave no fucks what anyone thought. I spent all my time chasing her, but every time I made my move, she would shut me down. She would come over every day to hang out at my house, but the second I got a little bit close, boom. Shot down again." Johnny wondered if he should be telling this story to someone after just making love, but Wrecker kept stroking his hair and back, so Johnny kept talking. "Finally, one day she was over at my house, as usual, and she was upset, but she wouldn't tell me why. This time, when I made my move, she came back at me just as hard. When it was over, I was like—this was a lot of work." Wrecker shook with laughter. Johnny couldn't stop. "No. Seriously. It was a lot of fucking work. Like, I had missed countless fun things with my friends trying to get with this girl and I had definitely pulled much harder orgasms on my own. It had not been worth it at all. Mostly, it had just been awkward, and she did not seem into it in the least. I thought, is this really what all the fuss has been about? Not long after that, I moved to L.A. and fell into my role as Jessie's night guard. Jessie put me in charge of watching Ezra, and he was battling anorexia at the time, so I felt an extra responsibility to always be there. I just fell into my place. It was a nice, quiet, and peaceful life."

Wrecker paused mid-stroke of Johnny's hair. "Wait. Are you saying that one time with that one girl is the only person you've ever been with?"

Johnny wasn't a blusher, but he felt his face heat at the question. "Yes. I was just happier alone until I met you."

"Huh," Wrecker said, sounding thoughtful as he went back to stroking Johnny. "What happened to the girl?"

A laugh burst from Johnny before he could stop it. "She's been dating my sister the past six years."

"Are you shitting me?" Wrecker asked on a snort.

Johnny tilted his chin up and met Wrecker's laughing gaze. "It turns out, that's why she was upset that day. She had been coming over every day, trying to catch Jenny's attention, but Jenny wouldn't give her the time of day. After I left town, they ran into each other at a club one night. The rest is history. They've been together ever since."

A wicked light entered Wrecker's eyes. "So you let one girl ruin you for all others."

Even though it hadn't been a question, Johnny shook his head. "I let my life in Illinois break me from wanting to live. It wasn't until I met you and you started making me feel things that I didn't want to feel that I started thinking about life again. I love my mom, but she was never around. She was always traveling for work or traveling to take a break from working, and us—like she ever had to raise us." Even Johnny heard the bitterness in his voice and couldn't stop it from happening. "She left us in a house with hate-filled religious zealots and then wondered why we ran the second we turned eighteen. I didn't realize until I was gone from that influence how I had thought more about suicide than any one person should while growing up. They were always yelling and throwing things. Preaching and bitching. I couldn't breathe there. By the time I made it to L.A., I was exhausted. All I wanted was for it to be quiet. Jessie gave me that when he gave me a job." Johnny chewed his bottom lip. He didn't want to ruin their moment, but Wrecker was his best friend, and he needed him right now. He met Wrecker's stare. "Things don't feel quiet anymore in L.A. I moved there to find the fame that fell in my lap with Brett, but I'm not happy. Don't get me wrong, I don't mind doing the videos and I love singing with Jessie, but I don't like where this is headed. Nothing feels peaceful anymore."

Wrecker nodded along. There wasn't an ounce of judgment in his eyes. "Is that why you packed your things and left? Are you running away?"

Johnny shrugged. "I guess. I just want things to be quiet."

For a moment, Wrecker eyed Johnny in silence, as if working things out in his head. Johnny swore he knew the moment Wrecker came to some sort of decision. His intensity doubled. "Move in with me."

Johnny's lips parted in surprise, but he didn't know what to say.

Wrecker wasn't finished. "I'm being serious. Come live with me. I'll give you a quiet life filled with bursts of mind-blowing sex. You can keep doing your videos, if that's what makes you happy. But I'll be your buffer from Brett roping you into live events that disrupt your peace. I'll act the controlling lover who doesn't want you out of his sight. Brett already thinks I'm an asshole. He won't be surprised."

Johnny's smile grew. "You're such an amazing person, but no. I would never let people think badly of you."

Wrecker rolled, pinning Johnny beneath him. Johnny's body hummed—like recognizing only Wrecker knew how to please him. Unfortunately, Wrecker didn't look like he planned to make Johnny fly. Instead, he looked intense. "Was that a no to me playing the controlling lover or a no to moving in with me?"

Johnny realized Wrecker was serious. "Maybe I snore," Johnny hedged, buying time.

"I've slept with you. You don't. Not that it would matter, but you also don't hog the blankets or kick. In fact, we're pretty damn perfect together."

"Brett said you closed the coffeehouse to go to Illinois with me. You told me you had it covered." Johnny was still desperately trying to buy time to think.

"I did have it covered. I closed. Stop dodging the question. I can take no for an answer if you worried about hurting my feelings. Just don't dodge me."

Without thought, Johnny's hands found Wrecker's ass. He massaged, trying to pull the man closer. "It's not that. I want to say yes, but I'm starting to worry that I've had too much to drink, and I'll wake up tomorrow to realize this was all a dream."

Wrecker bent his head and bit Johnny's bottom lip, pulling a chuckle from Johnny. "See. You felt that. It's not a dream." Wrecker looked thoughtful for a second. "Unless you count that you're a dream come true for me. I want to be with you, even if you're telling everyone else that we're only roommates. In fact, it's scary as hell how badly I just want to be with you."

It felt like a lead weight dropped on Johnny's chest at the thought of telling anyone that. "I don't want that. You're mine. I want everyone to know it."

A smile exploded across Wrecker's face. He looked ridiculously happy. "Was that a yes? I heard a yes."

There was no way Johnny could say no in the face of Wrecker's joy. "Yes."

Wrecker's expression shifted, turning so sweet that Johnny could barely breathe. "I love you. I only had the one condom with me."

A burst of laughter took Johnny by surprise. He truly was happier with Wrecker than he had ever been in his life. "I guess we'll have to find other means of entertainment until we can get to the store or go home."

Wrecker cupped Johnny's face before dropping his head and touching his lips to Johnny's. "You're mine to protect now," he whispered between kisses, melting Johnny's heart. Johnny had genuinely never been made to feel this way before. He was a calm-natured person, but he wanted to jump on the bed and shout at the top of his lungs. Johnny couldn't explain what happened. He just woke up one day in love with someone he never expected. Johnny didn't want this to ever stop. He wouldn't let it stop.

NINE

JOHNNY'S FIRST LIVE SHOW WENT BETTER THAN Brett could have dreamed. Afterward, Jessie had immediately made himself scarce. He claimed to no longer relish the limelight and he didn't want to steal any of Johnny's thunder. He had made a bad pun of that last part. Brett appreciated the ridiculousness on such a stressful night. Brett should feel triumphant. For the most part, he did. It was just harder being surrounded by so many people in love than he expected. His first big YouTube success story had been Falcon Vaspiro, a street fighter who Brett never believed would be stricken with love. Then Falcon had met the most unlikely of men and fallen hard. Falcon was only one person in his circle. It wasn't hard to avoid Falcon's overwhelming happiness.

Brett had simply stopped associating with the man unless they were working. Then Ezra had fallen, and Brett's circle had gotten a little smaller. Love had gotten harder to avoid. Johnny falling had been the ultimate blow. Johnny hadn't fallen in love with some random person and given Brett the choice to only see him while working. Nope. Johnny had fallen in love with the person Brett had always thought would be his. Brett's circle closed, leaving him alone.

As Brett looked on, Johnny smiled and chatted with reporters while Wrecker stood behind Johnny and pulled Johnny's hair up and into a bun. Such an intimate gesture showed how comfortable they were together. Wrecker kissed the side of Johnny's neck. Brett's eyes closed against the sight. They were real and happy.

"Pretty. Spoiled. Slightly bitchy. Now I'm adding 'tired' to the list of adjectives that come to mind when I think of you."

Brett's eyes shot open. A face he hadn't seen in ages stared back at him. Hazel eyes. Long blond hair. Body made for sin. "Roman? What are you doing here?"

A sexy smirk pulled at Roman's lips. "I can't believe you remembered my name."

"Why wouldn't I?" Brett asked with a nervous laugh.

Roman shrugged. He pulled his hair up and secured it with a rubber band from his wrist. Brett fought a snort. Roman's knowing smile never faltered. He knew everyone watched him. "I don't know. You just don't strike me as the type to remember anyone's name five minutes after meeting them." Before Brett could think of a response to that dickish comment, Roman moved on. "Falcon loves you. This is your new client's big night. Surely you didn't think he would miss it. I tagged along. You know, free trip to California and all that."

Brett fought an eye roll. "Yeah, being the best friend of Falcon's husband has really paid off for you."

Roman's smile grew. He snapped his fingers before pointing at Brett. "See. There's the slight bitchiness I was talking about. Little do you know, that shit turns me on."

Perplexed didn't begin to describe Brett when Roman was around. "Really, though. What are you doing here?"

"I told you. We came to see you. Some people recognized Falcon and he got held up, signing shit and taking pics. I slipped away and beat him to you."

Roman's gaze dropped to Brett's toes before slowly inspecting his body. He finally met Brett's stare again. "You know me. I like having you to myself." Roman reached up, flexing all the way, and worked the rubber band loose from his hair. Brett looked away. Johnny and Wrecker were finally alone. Wrecker kissed every spot on Johnny's face but his lips, making Johnny roar with laughter.

"Goddamn. Is that Wrecker Lewis? Lucky bastard."

Brett's gaze snapped back to Roman at the comment. Roman's gaze was still locked on Brett. "Which one?"

At his question, a sexy smile slowly stretched Roman's lips. "Me."

Roman always confused the fuck out of him. "Why you?"

"Because if they're busy, then I have you all to myself."

Brett shook his head. Even though he knew this was an act, and Roman made a living flirting with people, Brett wasn't immune. He hated that. It was always this way when they spoke. Roman flirted. Brett retreated to save himself. Tonight was no different. Brett forced himself to eye the lingering crowd, looking for Falcon. Only reporters, stagehands, and people with backstage passes remained. Still, there were a lot of people. Unfamiliar faces.

"Either you don't like me or you think I'm full of shit. I can never decide which it is," Roman said, pulling Brett's attention back his way, as if determined to have it.

"Maybe it's both." He watched the light leave Roman's eyes and immediately wanted it back. "Or it's neither," he added, scratching to get Roman back to being Roman. "Flirting with people is your forte. I know you don't mean anything you say to anyone, so it's hard to take you seriously. That doesn't mean I don't like you or that I think you're a liar. It just means I'm not interested in a bullshitter. L.A. is full of fake people who never mean what they say. If you take a look at my client list, you'll see they all have one characteristic in common. They're genuine. It's a trait I value."

The longer Brett spoke, the larger Roman's smile grew until his eyes shone bright with laughter. He shook his head. "You really are completely clueless, aren't you?"

Brett blinked at the insult. "Wow. I'm so glad I took the time to explain myself. I have to go." He tried stepping around Roman.

Roman touched his arm, stopping him. Their gazes met. Brett swore electricity raced through him, making his heart beat faster. "Falcon came all this way to see you. Don't run away yet." At the reminder, Brett blinked, coming back to reality. Before he could experience an iota of disappointment over Roman not stopping him for himself, Roman leaned closer and lowered his voice. "Plus, I'm not finished with you yet. I'm dead set on having your fire in my bed, so don't leave now. Stay and play."

Brett couldn't look away from Roman's lips. They were nice. Brett bet a lot of people had tasted them. He didn't know why he didn't walk away and find Falcon for himself. Brett didn't need to listen to this. He kind of wanted to, though. Johnny didn't need him. Wrecker had him. Falcon was apparently tied up with fans. They had a minute. "Oh, darling. I'm nowhere near that easy."

The smile that Roman wore spoke volumes. He was certain he had already won. Brett would play. He needed the distraction. In fact, Brett had a feeling this had been a long time coming. Maybe he would spend a long time coming. It wasn't like Brett had anything else to do. This didn't matter at all. It was a dalliance. Roman had no shot at stealing Brett's heart. None whatsoever.

THE PRIDE IN WRECKER'S CHEST KEPT swelling. It got bigger by the second. Johnny had looked sexy as fuck on that stool on stage with multicolored lights highlighting his features. Every time Johnny sang, he gave Wrecker chills. He was amazing and he belonged to Wrecker. With the show over, it was Wrecker's time to take care of what belonged to him.

"I promised to be the one who always brings you peace. To that end, ta-da." Wrecker led Johnny onto the roof of The Back Porch where he had enlisted Ezra's help to spread out a thick blanket and leave a packed ice chest. A few pillows littered the blanket. Ezra had done a beautiful job.

Johnny looked blown away. "Damn. I didn't even know you could come up here like this. How did you pull this off?"

"I have my ways," Wrecker said, trying to sound mysterious. He walked backward, holding Johnny's hand and luring him toward the waiting picnic. "You didn't eat anything before the show. I know it was nerves, but I can't have that. So I'm giving you the night sky, the stars, peace, and food."

"What about you? Are you part of the bargain?"

At Johnny's question, Wrecker stopped walking and let Johnny close the gap between them. "You've always had me." Wrecker claimed Johnny's mouth, driving his point home. No one had ever had Wrecker the way Johnny did. They were more than a team. Wrecker could never think of a good enough label for them. They lived together, but it didn't sound like enough to say they were dating or a couple. For Wrecker, they were a dream come true.

Johnny didn't stop at a simple kiss. He tried getting even closer. With no clue how it happened, Wrecker ended up on his back with Johnny straddling his body. Johnny bit and sucked, stealing Wrecker's breath and every thought from his head. Johnny kept moving against him, making Wrecker burn.

"You were the only face I could see in that crowd tonight," Johnny said as he leaned away only long enough to steal Wrecker's shirt. He returned and licked Wrecker's nipple. Wrecker's back arched. Johnny's teeth scraped the hardened bud, sending tingles down Wrecker's spine. Johnny knew how to drive Wrecker crazy.

"I'm supposed to be taking care of you." Wrecker wasn't complaining. It was just that he needed to know Johnny was fed and cared for.

Johnny chuckled against Wrecker's skin as he popped the button on Wrecker's jeans. "You are taking care of me. I need to lick your cock. See? Needs being met," he growled as he set Wrecker's erection free.

Wrecker took a steadying breath as Johnny kissed a path down his body. Johnny was unlike anyone Wrecker had ever met. He didn't play games or pretend he didn't have needs. Johnny told Wrecker what he wanted without shame and then took it with even less guilt. It was hotter than touching the sun. Johnny always kept Wrecker so ramped that Wrecker had been having to find creative ways to keep Johnny pleasured because Wrecker never lasted as long as he would like once Johnny got ahold of him.

Johnny's hot breath brushed Wrecker's dick. His tongue barely flickered across Wrecker's crown. Johnny's phone chirped with an incoming message. "Fuck," Johnny growled, sitting back on his heels.

Wrecker thought he might cry as he watched Johnny dig out his phone. "Are you seriously answering that right now?"

An evil-sounding chuckle rumbled from Johnny as he stared at his phone. "It's my sister, congratulating us."

Wrecker tried to think straight with his dick throbbing. "You were amazing. There's no denying that." Wrecker was dying for him to be even more amazing and put the phone away before Wrecker was forced to jack off on the roof of his coffeehouse.

"Not me. Well, she said that too, but us." He turned the phone where Wrecker could see it. Wrecker had to force his eyes to focus on the device. There was a picture of them together after the show. They were staring at each other with so much love that, even knowing how much they loved each other, the picture still took Wrecker's breath. Then he read the headline. "YouTube star Johnny Savage announces his engagement to boyfriend 'Wrecker' Lewis."

Wrecker took the phone from Johnny and read the headline three more times before focusing on Johnny. Rage killed his lust. "This is from reporter you talked to for a long time after the show. What the fuck? Why would she do this?" It had been Johnny's big night. His big moment, and the first article about it was how Johnny was dating a man. Not just dating but engaged. It wasn't even a real headline. Wrecker was apoplectic. He wanted to burn something to the ground.

Despite Wrecker's growing rage, Johnny never stopped smiling. "She asked about us when you went to grab me a bottle of water. I told her we're getting married soon."

Wrecker blinked. He didn't think he heard Johnny right. "I'm sorry, what?"

Johnny took the phone from him and set it aside. With nothing in his way, Johnny leaned in and kissed Wrecker. It was sweet and distracting. Wrecker almost forgot what they were discussing until Johnny picked up the threads of their conversation. "I figured if you say no to my proposal, then no one would probably think anything about it. We're just dating and maybe having a super long engagement. But if you say yes, then there's no chance of some other reporter taking the story and turning it ugly. That lady was nice. Brett said she would write a professional and positive story about us." Johnny went back to kissing his way down Wrecker's body.

Wrecker cupped Johnny's jaw and forced his gaze back to his. "Whoa. Whoa. Whoa. Wait. You haven't asked me anything."

A slow smile spread across Johnny's face. "I

know, Mr. Impatient." Johnny sat back on his heels again and reached into his shirt pocket. He pulled out a ring that Wrecker couldn't see many details about in the dark. He didn't need to see the details. Johnny had that fucking ring in his pocket all night. At some point, he had made a special trip to get it. In the three months they had been living together, they hadn't once discussed marriage. Wrecker couldn't breathe.

Johnny stared at the band he held between his thumb and forefinger. "I didn't actually know if I should buy a ring or what I should say after I did. Truthfully, I've been carrying it everywhere for the past two weeks." Johnny's gaze moved to Wrecker's. "Maybe it took me a lot longer to find myself than most people, and maybe I still don't know what I'm doing half the time, but I know wherever I'm headed or whatever I'm doing, I want to do it with you. I feel like an idiot a lot. While everyone else just fits in naturally, I don't. Just like when I started coming here, everyone avoided me except for you. I don't think I fit anyplace I go, but I fit with you. Even once I knew I wanted to marry you, I didn't know how to do this part. I've driven myself crazy, wondering should I drop to one knee or if I should ask if this is something you even want, but I know that you're who I want." Johnny didn't have an ounce of doubt in his eyes. He took an audible breath. "Wrecker, I love you. Will you—"

Wrecker exploded into action, taking Johnny to the ground. He tucked the man beneath him and kissed him, cutting off the question before Johnny could ask. It turned out, he didn't need to be asked. In his heart, he had always known it was only a matter of time. They were meant to be. If there was a step beyond being married, Wrecker wanted it. He wanted to own Johnny so irrecoverably that no one ever even looked their way again. Wrecker tore at Johnny's clothes, needing to be closer.

"Is that a yes?"

Wrecker snatched the ring from Johnny and shoved it on his finger without answering. The time for talking was done. Now was the time for action. He needed to be as close as possible to Johnny. No barriers. Soon enough, they could rush to whatever union Johnny wanted. Wrecker's heart wasn't soothed until their bare skin touched. Then it was like his entire body sighed. Wrecker kissed Johnny. He poured his heart and soul into the man he loved, hoping Johnny could feel his total adoration. They had met in this building because of someone else's engagement. It felt right that they should seal their love here. On the roof of Wrecker's second dream, and on the night Johnny fulfilled his lifelong desire, they became something new. Neither of them had expected to end up here, yet they had. It just went to show that no one really knew what their perfect life looked like until they had it. Wrecker only knew one thing for sure. He loved this man. Wrecker would never stop showing him. This was forever.

KEEP AN EYE OUT FOR THE NEXT CANDIED Crush, *Beautifully Stolen*. Brett and Roman were first introduced in *Salty Baby*, but you don't need to have read that book to enjoy theirs.

Please consider leaving a review at the retailer where you purchased this book. Reviews really help with a book's visibility, which allows me to continue writing more stories. Thank you, Charity.

ABOUT THE AUTHOR

Charity Parkerson is an award winning and multi-published author with several companies. Born with no filter from her brain to her mouth, she decided to take this odd quirk and insert it in her characters.

*Eight-time Readers' Favorite Award Winner
   *2015 Passionate Plume Award Finalist
   *2013 Reviewers' Choice Award Winner
   *2012 ARRA Finalist for Favorite Paranormal Romance
   *Five-time winner of The Mistress of the Darkpath

Connect with her online:

—Sign up for my newsletter: http://bit.ly/CharityNews
   —Join my readers' group on Facebook: http://bit.ly/CharitysTribe
   —Website: charityparkerson.com

—Facebook: facebook.com/authorCharityParkerson

facebook.com/TheMenofSin

—Twitter: twitter.com/CharityParkerso

—Instagram: Instagram.com/sinnerauthor

www.ingramcontent.com/pod-product-compliance
Lightning Source LLC
Chambersburg PA
CBHW060228180626
46813CB00007B/2998